# Prologue

The old land rover rattled along the Afr
only way to describe the journey for thi
style with most roads rough and bumpy and the fact that the Land
Rover was still running was a miracle in itself. The British Sanctions
had prevented any vehicle spare parts coming to Ian Smith's
independent Rhodesia. consequently, to get spare parts for
vehicles it was necessary to cannibalise them from a similar
vehicle which wasn't being used Now. After 10years there were
no more Land Rovers left to cannibalise. Tom McClelland had
managed, with the aid of his African mechanic who being unable
to cannibalise any more vehicles, was able to make new parts for
the McClelland vehicle with apparent ease and to keep the vehicle
on the road for nearly 30 years the latest 10 of those being since
Ian Smith's attempted independence and the British sanctions to
make him unpopular with the people of Rhodesia. Therefore, no
new parts from abroad were available.

The McClelland's were old Africa. Tom's great grandfather had
ridden with Jameson into what was then Matabele land. The
grandfather ended up owning vast areas of top farmland rather
than becoming involved in the mining industry. Elgin farm a gift
from his grandfather was now Tom's pride and joy and he had
become a very good farmer as well.

Together with Tom McClelland there were four other people in
the car, and all were gloriously happy for this was the week
before Christmas and three of the occupants were teenagers
returning from their boarding school Victoria McClelland Tom's
wife sat in front with him. At forty she remained the vivacious
blond that Tom had married twenty years before. Her skin still
clear and unwrinkled despite the strong African sun

a complete contrast to her husband who was knarled and wrinkled and looked much older than his forty-five years.

The McClelland children sat side by side in the back. John a tall slight 17-year-old, with his father's red hair and his mother's slim build.

 He was already popular with the girls and was really enjoying life.

Jeanie his sister, just 16, and already a stunning blond a picture of her mother and fully aware of the effect she had on the schoolboys and even on many older boys and men as well next to her sat Robert Markham. Fully aware of Jeannie's charms which brushed against his as the Land Rover bounced over the rutted track. Jeanie knowing what was happening took care to press her leg against Robert from time to time and to turn and smile. Robert felt himself redden each time and tried to think of things other than the soft pressure against his leg. The Markham's who owned the farm next to the McClelland's. In a country where distance didn't seem to matter were at twenty miles away considered to be neighbours the result of this meant that the families became good friends who enjoyed helping each when they could. This resulted in what was happening on this occasion because one of their ways of helping each other was to take it in turn to collect each other's children from the nearest rail station when the children returned for holidays from their schools in South Africa.

Thanks to attempted independence by Ian Smith and his government this was not an easy time for farmers in Rhodesia. Sanctions had taken their toll, while Smith's attempted independence had also caused the danger from terrorist bands to develop and over the years greatly increase. Neither the

McClelland's nor the Markham's had so far ever been bothered by terrorists but both farmhouses and barns were surrounded by strong security fences. This resulted in both families having a relaxed view on matters. Their African workers were very happy, well paid, had access to medical facilities and education for their children. Consequently, attack by their own workers was very unlikely. There was also the advantage that both farms were far away from the normal terrorist routes and activities. Precautions however dictated that the Land Rover contained three pistols, one for Victoria who was a crack shot and one each for the children who were also very good shots. There was also a former British .303 rifle, and a pump action shotgun. In addition, John had lying at his feet a British Stirling submachine gun,

Tom McClelland was not about to give up easily to terrorists. Robert Markham was also a reasonable shot with a pistol, but his strength lay in his rifle shooting

which was second to none and had won him a number of trophies at school as also had his sword fencing abilities. Robert was also very successful in his lessons, studying hard and doing well in his exams.

The Land Rover was turning now through two open gates into the compound that lay in front of the Markham bungalow.

Robert thought it seemed noticeably quiet but then it was late morning, and the workers would be in the fields not the farmyard. He jumped down from the Land Rover, fetched his bag from the back seat and said his thank you to the McClelland's

"Tell your dad I'll be over next week to see him and that I've found a bottle of Talisker, don't forget we are going out into the bush it's time you put your shooting talents to good use ." said Tom McClelland.

"see you next week Robert, good bye gorgeous." Jeannie called and blew Robert a kiss. Reddening him yet again and made Her mum Victoria laughingly shout out, "leave the boy alone,"

Robert ran up the steps into the house calling out," Mum! Mum! It's me I'm home." Still no sound and even more strange no greeting from Oudbass the families' aging mongrel dog, a cross between a Rhodesian Ridgeback and a Great Dane.

Robert continued through the house heading for the kitchen still calling out. Mum  and Dad. Now he was becoming concerned, it was quiet, too quiet. Making him think that something must be wrong. He realised that something was definitely  wrong. When he heard from behind himself a low whimpering sound of a dog coming from his parent's bedroom. Quickly he turned running back the way he had come, past the front door  and through the hall, he now could hear the whimpering noise much louder.

Then he saw the first body. That of an African dressed only in shorts, lying partly across the doorway of his parent's bedroom. This caused him to slow as the full horror hit him, the farm had been attacked that's why it was so quiet. The unarmed workers frightened by what was happening must have run off into the bush to hide for safety. Robert stepped over the body and through the doorway seeing the bedroom was in chaos with chairs toppled over and papers on the floor. Then he saw Oudbass the dog was lying whimpering in pain in a corner near the window, Robert saw the dog try to wag its tail at seeing him

Robert was now close enough to see one leg of the dog had been almost severed by a machete blow, another cut across the dog's back  had left it almost paralysed.

Then the full horror-struck Robert, in the furthest corner of the room lay his mother and father propped against the wall.

Where they had been shot and slashed with machetes, at the sight of this Robert was sick and He reeled over against the door, holding on to it to keep himself standing. Furniture had been overturned and broken; two more Africans lay dead in the room. His father's pistol was lying inches from his lifeless right hand, his left arm was around his wife's shoulders her head lying against it .Almost severed by a cut across her neck.

Again, Oudbass whimpered, and Robert startled out of his horror Walked forward to pick up his father's pistol which he raised and closing on the dog fired to end Oudbass's agony the pistol shot sounded loud and clear across the bush. Tom McClelland slammed on the brakes, bringing the Land Rover to a shuddering dusty halt, before saying, "pistols everybody! Victoria take the shotgun and John the 303. as well." Quickly the family prepared with a smoothness and speed that came only because of past practice. One of tom's simple precautions was to be prepared for an attack on the farm or the Land Rover and that had meant practice after practice. While the family prepared their weapons, the Land Rover was quickly turned and raced back the way it had come, each family member armed and ready, yet frightened, frightened for themselves, frightened for the Markham's, frightened of the unknown, for none of them had ever shot at another human being before. They found Robert sitting at the top of the steps of the bungalow.

He had been sick again and now face in his hands was quietly crying. The two females ran to him while Tom and John cautiously went up the steps into the bungalow, weapons ready. Seeing them arrive Robert shouted,

"They are in the bedroom" "Mum and dad are there dead," Then he fell silent, tears streaking his dusty cheeks. Tom McClelland spoke to Victoria, saying, "leave Jeannie to see to Robert, get on the radio to Harare get support up here, they might get the bastards before they have gone too far and you must keep a sharp look out because they could come back. Then please radio our farm, warn Tawanda our workers leader to prepare, in case the killers could be heading our way, if he gets the workmen armed and organised, they'll fight." Tom led the way to the Markham's bedroom, John just behind him, a glance through the door told Tom all he needed to know but he forced himself to check the bodies just in case there was a chance of life. John got no further than the door when the smell of sick and blood made him vomit. His father grim faced now put an arm around his son, "steady! Deep breaths and remember we must stay alert the bastards could come back and it will be an hour before Help gets here". They moved slowly checking each room in turn finding another African dead in the kitchen, his face neck and arms savaged and covered in bite marks, Oudbass had done his work well, if in vain and given the Markham's some warning. Outside lay two more dead Africans and someway away in front of the stables lay the body of Harry Markham, Robert's twenty-year-old brother and those of three more Africans. An SLR rifle lay beside Harry its stock broken, an empty magazine on the ground another in the rifle. The body had been badly slashed. It seemed that when he ran out of ammunition the terrorists had decided to finish the job with machetes, the broken rifle showed this had not been an easy job for them Within twenty minutes of finding the bodies the McClelland's had again radioed for help, Harry's body had been taken inside for safety and the bungalow doors closed. Then they were on their way heading for their own farm, a tearful broken-hearted Robert safely in the back of the Land Rover, this time between the two women while John drove and Tom sat cradling the Stirling machine gun on his lap, fear oozed from every pore, what would they find at Elgin their home farm. When Victoria had radioed all had been well. Tom had spoken to Tawanda who was in charge of the farm workers and although he reassured Victoria and Tom that all was well, uncertainty still remained in them. 15minutes later two helicopters appeared, they circled overhead for a quick look at the Land Rover then flew on towards the Markham's farm. Tom McClelland again radioed to his own farm discovering all was OK. Next, he radioed Bulawayo to try to get a radio frequency for the helicopters but to no avail, they were military and would deal with the problem without discussing it with anyone. He was also told that he should get home and prepare his defences. Robert was quiet throughout the journey, he had stopped crying and just sat stiffly between the two females neither of which had been allowed to view the carnage inside the bungalow, but both had cried for this boy who had seen such terrible things and Victoria wondered how it would affect him. Tom McClelland's farm had been spared any attack. Their losses suffered at Markham's farm may have frightened off the terrorists or more likely they were Heading back to some places of safety anyway and had dispersed after the attack. The Rhodesian troops had helicoptered in and set about tracking them, sending other troops to try to get ahead but nothing was found and no one was caught. That night after refusing to eat, Robert was put to bed but couldn't sleep. He lay quietly thinking, sometimes about school, sometimes about hunting with his father and sometimes about his mother working in the kitchen baking fresh bread, also sometimes about Harry his older brother. He had so admired Harry. Who reminded him very much of his father due to Harry's strength and shooting accuracy and knowledge of the bush and also his ability to travel through it, live and hunt in it. This was as well as Harry's very good ability and knowledge of how to farm both animals and plants.

Harry who wanted to join the Selous Scouts. The southern Rhodesian antiterrorist military regiment the equivalent to the SAS in their training. Big strong, silent Harry, Robert's slightly older brother, who took after their father. Robert also sometimes thought just about Africa, he so liked this continent, yet it had taken everything else he loved and destroyed them. With the death of his family only Rhodesia was left that he cared for and enjoyed. It was about 11:30pm. when he heard the soft knock on his bedroom door, then it was opened. Jeannie came into the room, "I couldn't sleep and saw the light under your door, I hope you don't mind if I come in?" He sat up, acutely aware that he was completely naked under the covers,

"No! No! of course I don't mind" he said, "I just can't sleep, I keep on thinking of so many things, my mind just won't settle." Jeannie sat on the edge of the bed, saying, "It must have been awful for you Robert. Seeing that room and what was in it, our father described it to us and even then, it was horrible."

Tears again rolled down Robert's cheeks and Jeannie reached across, put an arm around Him and held him tight and close. After a while he stopped crying and became aware of the soft warmth of this young girl. He smelled a freshness off her, a cleanness and he also felt her skin against his cheek where her dressing gown had fallen open. Nuzzling closer now he brushed against her young body and slowly brought his hand up to gently stroke the back of her head feeling his hand touching her hair and in response felt her tighten her grip Pulling him closer, now she was kissing his hair and his neck and he stretched his head up to face her. She kissed him full on the lips pressing tightly, then her tongue was brushing against his and now against his lips and inner cheeks. He responded pushing his own tongue inside her mouth. His hand stroking gently down her neck made her sigh. Her own hand now moved across his bare chest stroking his nipples  She fell back now pulling him alongside herself, he heard her sigh with pleasure,  She was now reponding to his upset by cuddleing him and he responded by cuddling her but didn't wish to go any further as he had no wish to upset Jeannie or her parents

They lay together for what seemed a long time, She stroked his back and he quietly almost reverently kissing her face and her neck,

Jeannie felt very careing, she had played the woman's part and brought comfort to this young man, Gently she eased Robert off her and onto his back, now it was her turn to return to her own bedroom slowly she rose off the bed and left Roberts bedroom swithching off the light as she went Jeanie continued to join Robert each night as the days went by and gave him a few kisses and a cuddle to try and keep him as happy as possible. Then five days later Robert returned to his parent's farm which was his now. To his surprise and pleasure, Everything had been tidied up. Unknown to Robert, Jeannie's father Tom McClelland who had been Robert's father's best friend, had, since the terror attack, taken over the running of things at the Markham's farm to keep the farm and it's workers in good order. Robert entered the house, walking from room to room of what had been his home, he couldn't bear to enter his parent's bedroom in which their bodies had lain when he first saw them dead. Instead he strolled slowly through the house looking into the lounge, the kitchen, his own room, his brother's room, he nearly broke down at this point but kept going. Now he was in his father's study, books and papers strewn across the desk, just as it always had been, A wooden box also lay open at one side, in it were the family passports and personal papers, he picked up each passport in turn looking first at his mother's photograph then his father's again almost crying. Finally he found his brother Harry's passport then he leafed through the other papers in the box, birth certificates medical forms and his parents' marriage licence as well as his brother Harry's personal papers. He left almost everything as it was. His father's brother who lived in England Would hopefully soon arrive to take over the farm and settle matters, as there were no other relations. Robert left only almost everything as he had found it, except he put his brother Harry's passport and birth certificate in his pocket together with Harry's other personal papers. The next day Robert's parent's and his Brother Harry's bodies were brought back to the farm from the place where they had been kept until after the coroner's report. Here on the farm, they were to be buried. Following this awful day for him, Robert returned to the McClelland's farm where he had been living. That night Jeanie again came to Robert's room and they again had their usual session of love making. The next night Robert didn't wait for Jeannie to come to his room but went to hers, there he made love to her quickly, brutally almost, then he kissed her goodbye let himself out of the house and drove off in his parent's old Cherokee station wagon. Two weeks in Bulawayo and Robert now calling himself Harry Markham. Went on to try to join the Selous Scouts. Nine months later unknown to Robert, a baby boy was born on Elgin farm.

Robert having his dead brother Harry's passport as well as Harry's other paperwork.  Pretended to be his brother Harry and went to join the Selous Scouts

# Chapter One

Having left his friend's house and taken with himself all of his brother Harry's certificates including his brothers membership details of joining the Selous Scouts and his birth certificate and passport. Robert Markham who looked very like his brother Harry and was a very well built 18 year old. Prepared to become his brother Harry and join the Selous scouts as an officer Just as his brother had already done. Robert now calling himself Harry, went on to fulfil his own dream of joining the Selous Scouts. Even if it was by cheating through pretending to be his brother Harry. The Selous scouts were recruited from volunteers less than 30 years old who demonstrated they were very tough and loyal, also with maturity, intelligence and professionalism. Robert Now calling himself Harry and pretending to be twenty which had been his brother Harry's age was taken on as a member of the Selous Scouts without any problem. Helped by all the paperwork he had taken from his former home which was accepted by the people he had to speak to in order to join the Selous Scouts. He now had to carry out the beginner's training as his brother Harry had not actually been to the camp, so he now had to go through the preparation and so become a full member in his own right even if he was pretending to be his brother. Fortunately for Robert, Harry had been through the selection tests at the selection camp called Wafa-Wafa, near to the shore of lake Kariba to the north of Rhodesia. This meant that as he was pretending to be Harry, Robert didn't need to do the selection tests. This was lucky for him as only 15% ever qualified. With his knowledge of the Shona language Robert understood that the name Wafa Wafa meant, they die that die, those who remain behind remain behind. The selection tests and preparation courses were based on those of the British SAS as the commandant was Lieutenant colonel Francis Reid- Daly, A former member of the British SAS. Now Robert acting as Harry was to be introduced to the Selous Scout's barracks at Andre Rabie, their motto Pamwe Chete meaning altogether (working as a team} Robert  to be called Harry from here onwards discovered the Selous Scout methods of controlling terrorism involved being trained by men who had been former terrorists themselves which enabled them to know how to infiltrate enemy terrorist groups by joining them and then at times turning on them, taking them by surprise and therefore killing large numbers. They also let the enemy know of Selous Scout's hidden camps. Then knowing the terrorists would try to sneak up on them to make an attack.  The Selous Scouts would have guards hiding in the bush a little distance from the camp. These guards could radio the camp if they saw the terrorists coming and enable a successful ambush to be  carried out when the terrorists tried to sneak up on the camps.  Harry found his training also involved completing a very difficult assault course which involved a high fitness level and the ability to cope with very high heights. He also had to complete Parachuting which involved learning how to land properly by facing the wind and rolling over sideways and then getting up quickly and running around his parachute to prevent the wind and parachute pulling him across the ground. Also how to leave the plane properly, his body saucer shaped head raised and with arms and legs straight and spread out so as to keep himself stable as he fell waiting for the chute to open properly. His first jump was frightening for him, as it was for almost everybody. Not just because he was warned along with 5 others on the plane that once the door was opened to let them out, they must be careful not to allow any ripcords to be accidently pulled because this would cause the released parachute to be pulled by the wind out of the plane through the open door.  The wearer with it, who could then possibly be caught on the tail wing of the plane which meant the plane couldn't land without killing the wearer. What was frightening was the open door and the sight of the ground five thousand feet below with the wind blowing in through the open door as the plane flew along. Harry's first jump went well from his point of view, when he jumped out he thought he had been stable with his body saucer shape, arms outstretched and legs apart. he had made his count and only became upright as the parachute opened after he had counted out loud, "one thousand, two thousand, three thousand, four thousand and five thousand, so that he had remained stable for 5 seconds until his chute opened fully. He then straightened up when the chute fully opened.  He was now able to pull a few cords on the chute as he had been instructed to do and so steered himself to the proper landing spot. Where he landed using the method he was taught during training. Which was to be sure to turn and face the wind and as his feet touched the ground to bend his knees and roll over sideways then immediately to jump up and quickly run around the parachute so as the cords would stop the wind pulling it and dragging him over the ground. He was then approached by his trainer and told he had done very well for a first jump and he could if he wished try 3 more jumps that day and would receive a full report on paper. Which would be left at his living area in the camp that evening. Following  his three jumps and feeling quite tired due to the pressure involved, Harry quickly went to his living quarters to have a quick meal and a drink before going to bed where he read his Jump report, which said to his surprise the following, "First  jump, began looking down, you made a loud count of five seconds and you managed to stay stable until your chute opened properly, even though your legs were a little bent and kicking, otherwise you were good, including your landing. Second jump, good saucer shape, although head looking down, arms and legs stretched out and steady, loud five second count, exit position very stable then another good landing. Third jump, good exit, saucer shape, head looking forward, arms and legs in good positions, body stable and good loud counting. Also a very good landing.  Three jumps and good improvement in each one, very well done.  Three more good jumps and the way could be open for you to be allowed to make an attempt at a free fall jump."

 His next training was on the following day and was to be, how to use the Military weapons.  He was already a very good shot with a rifle and hit the target accurately each time. this led to him receiving praise from the trainer and encouragement to spend his time practicing with his pistol until he became as good a shot with that as he was with the rifle. this was something he was pleased to carry out. He was now to be also introduced to explosives including hand grenades and do it yourself bombs. Followed by how to use a bayonet before being introduced to the use of A large machine gun called a Bren gun placed on it's legs before firing and also how to hold and fire a handheld smaller machine gun. He was also introduced to both the Selous Scout weapons and those used by the terrorists taken from those who had been captured or killed. These enemy weapons might have to be used sometimes in emergencies. Due to his high motivation to become a Selous Scout and pay back the terrorists for what they did to his family. Together with his tough upbringing by his father. His high level of intelligence and his understanding of how to survive the Difficulties of the Rhodesian bush. His ability to be a good team member and his knowledge of how to obtain food from the bush or when needed, create somewhere to live in the bush, Robert now acting as his brother Harry, was readily accepted as a volunteer to the Selous Scouts. Some Selous Scouts were also very skilful horse men which was not one of Harry's strong points although he had spent some time riding when having a break from his school and riding on his family farm, he had not ridden enough to get to really know horses and feel confident in their use  however he worked hard with his training in basic combat skills including completing the very difficult assault course and practicing it until he could handle it very well especially the high parts which included dragging himself along a single length of rope held high between two metal poles, part of sets of metal steps. he also endured mounting a 1ofoot high wall aided by another man as well as springing to catch the top on his own and then pulling himself up and over it he also had to take part in night training.  On one day was able to complete a 62 mile march, carrying a pack weighing 66pounds and finishing the distance with an act of very fast marching. He was also given training in how to pretend to be a guerrilla himself so that he could at a later point, together with other Selous Scouts pretend to be part of the guerrillas and gain intelligence about them. To enable them to carry this out members of the Selous Scouts were trained to work as small undercover teams, able to travel in the forests and pass themselves off as the rebel guerrillas. Harry joined in with this aspect of the training with his usual enthusiasm although he knew that being white, he would never be able to pass off as a rebel and join a small undercover team and pretend to be a member of the guerrillas, even if he could travel like them through the bush. Learning how the Selous Scouts acted towards the terrorists was also very acceptable to him as a result of his anger at terrorists and his desire for revenge. Harry as Robert was now called would still have the opportunity even as a none riding member of the Selous Scouts, to use his shooting and bush living ability to help reduce the numbers of Rhodesian Zanla rebels behaving as terrorists and attacking from camps in other countries such as Mozambique. Having completed all of his training, Harry on an early occasion was made the leader of a team of 40 Selous Scouts who were sent to Mozambique to raid a guerrilla camp. This camp had been previously inspected by other members of the Selous Scouts who dressed in every day clothes had sneaked into Mozambique and pretended to want to join the guerrillas, after spending some time in the camp they left to return to Rhodesia pretending they were going back as guerrillas. A new team of Selous Scouts led by Harry next approached the camp and were equipped to deal with the numbers in it and any security arrangements that there were, they also approached at night hoping the darkness would help them to succeed in their plan to wipe out the terrorists living in the camp. The camp consisted of five wooden dormitories, one for the terrorist leaders. Three for the male terrorists and one for the female terrorists. The buildings were surrounded by individual stone walls and the whole camp by an electric barbed wire fence. There were no watching guards or towers except at the main entrance to the camp for it's protection. The Selous Scouts acting under Harry's instructions had brought with themselves wire cutters and long pieces of rubber covered wire so they could connect the barbed wire before cutting it by placing the rubber covered wire between where the cuttings would be made and keeping the fence connected and so not warn anybody the wire had been cut but making it easier to pass through, they also divided themselves into five groups each group to attack a specific dormitory and entered the camp. Each group fully armed approached it's set dormitory and quietly waited for the signal to attack, then getting the signal from a weak flash from a very dull torch held by Harry as arranged they opened the doors of each of the dormitories, entered and immediately shot every one they saw, within less than twenty minutes they had killed all of the guerrillas in the camp except for the females who came running out of their dormitory and shot the group appointed to deal with them and began firing at the others who dropped to the ground behind the dormitory outside walls and fired back eventually killing all of the females as well as several other terrorists who approached them from the tower at the main gate firing hand held machine guns. Fortunately Harry's men were all well protected by the walls around the dormitories so none of Harry's men were injured.

This situation had taken the four other teams by surprise and left them confused, what they didn't know was the group appointed to attack the female dormitory burst in like the others only to be confronted by twelve elderly smiling women and were unable to bring themselves to shoot and kill them, so turned and fled,  a few minutes later to be followed by twelve women all armed with rifles and machine pistols firing at them and killing all but one who later  explained to his angry comrades in the other four teams what had happened when his team entered their set dormitory. The final outcome of the completed attack by the Selous Scouts had been the loss of eight Selous Scouts and the death of fifty possible guerrillas. The Selous scouts quickly left the camp through the gap they had made when they entered. The hoped to quickly return through the bush to their own country. They left with a team of three of their own men who were very skilled in travelling through the bush, coming more slowly behind them to check if they were being followed by any forces who could possibly have caught up with them before they arrived safely back to their own country. This was so as to avoid any surprise attacks by other guerrillas or Mozambique military who might be following them. After a short time one of the three arrived at Harry's full squadron and told them that they were being followed by fifty guerrillas and Harry suggested that in case the followers caught up with them and attacked them from behind. Maybe they should find a place to set up a good ambush and remove them.   Which they managed to do, finding a place in the bush a little way from the track they were using, Where they could see the track clearly from a reasonable distance away on either side, so that when they started the ambush the enemy couldn't immediately attack them. Also the area alongside the track was covered by very thick tangled bush which would have made running through to attack them very difficult. They then continued further and left the track to circle round to where they intended to make the ambush and so prevent the followers from knowing they had left the track. Harry as their leader, divided them into three teams, one team of 20 to make the ambush and one team which would also make their way through the bush to wait further back along the track so as to stop the enemy fleeing that way and one further along the track to stop the enemy fleeing forward along the track. When the enemy followers arrived, the ambush took place and Harrys squadron of very good shots with half placed on either side of the track managed to remove a large number of the followers with their first shots, the remaining followers immediately tried to attack back but found it too difficult to get through the tangled bushes and so lay on the ground partly hidden by the bushes and firing back as best they could. Not being able to see them clearly because they were now lying down.  Harry then radioed the other two teams and suggested that they should sneak quietly along the track and shoot the enemy lying on the ground and his two ambush groups would then move down on the enemy as well, Once the enemy's attention was removed from the ambush groups. This proved to be very successful as the two teams arrived together and were able to shoot most of the remaining enemy lying along each side of the track and were then joined by Harry's men who coming through the bush from each side dealt with any enemy men who had crawled into the bush and had turned to fire at the arriving men on the track. With all of the enemy dead Harry got all of his men quickly together again none of which had been wounded or killed.  They then collected the weapons and ammunition as well as anything else of use from the bodies of the dead enemy. After doing this they quickly set off for their own country again arriving back safely. Once there, they reported to the Selous Scout leaders what had happened, explaining the mistake made by the group that had failed in it's attack on the women's dormitory and the consequences and asked that in future when possibly attacking  a group of women, a very unusual happening for soldiers, that men with special training and attitude would be sent. Harry Markham although not part of the group that made the mistake but having in mind the loss of his complete family put himself forward as a possible member of such a group, yet never again was placed in such a position. He then when taking part in other attacks on their enemies behaved as a very capable Selous Scout.  Partly because of his enthusiasm for killing terrorists and of his hard work during his Selous Scout training as well as his already very good shooting ability, his former experience of the Bush when growing up. Which Provided him with very good bush knowledge and capability.

His development as a Selous Scout was later to be very useful for Robert Markham now known as Harry Markham. Especially when he moved from Rhodesia to try to join the Australian SAS as Harry Markham. Later While still using the name of Harry, when he took upon himself his British job as a state assassin of terrorists and their leaders, his Selous Scout experiences also proved helpful. As a Selous Scout he knew about the attempted assassination of Joshua Nkomo although he himself was not part of that.  The Selous Scouts although famous for their use of horses and their special training of the horses for military use. The men had been trained like the British SAS by using a former British SAS officer. Harry also learned that The Selous scouts would use Terrorist type methods to counter enemy terrorists. They would insert, poisoned clothing, food, drink and medicine into the terrorist supply chain whenever possible. Also captured terrorists were kept in prison and promised a painful death unless they were prepared to provide the Selous scouts with information about their fellow terrorists. Together with what had happened to his family and his training with the Selous Scouts, Robert now to be known evermore as Harry had become a person lacking in gentle feelings towards those, whither young, old, male, or female, of colour or white, who hurt normal, gentle well behaved, loving people, although he himself would sometimes treat a person badly if it meant he was protecting lots of others. This all would be seen in his future behaviour, especially towards terrorists or those who were evil in their own behaviour or those who supported terrorists either by encouraging their terrorist behaviour or by providing finance for them or by smuggling weapons and explosives to them.

With the change of government in Rhodesia, in 1979 followed by the disbandment of the Selous Scouts in early 1980, Harry decided it was time he left what had become Zimbabwe for somewhere else. He thought of Britain but given that he had relations there who might want him to give up his military life and become more settled he thought he would try Australia First. He had heard about the Australian SAS and thought he might try to join them, if given the opportunity. He arranged to travel to Sydney in 1980 taking all of his dead brother's paperwork with him which proved him to be Harry Markham a white officer of the now world known Selous Scouts and the son of former British parents. He expected to be welcomed and so he was. He was able to make friends with some scuba divers and was able to carry out scuba diving as a hobby. He also was able to continue as a hobby, the sport of sword fencing which he had already enjoyed as a young boy whilst at school in South Africa. A sport he had been good at while at school. Shortly after he arrived in Sydney, he applied to join the Australian SAS. He was tested for the Australian SAS and proved to be very successful at what he was expected to know and be able to do, due to his background in the Selous Scouts where he had been trained by a former member of the British SAS. The result being that he was given a lieutenant's rank. Whilst working with the Australian SAS Harry's knowledge of explosives was greatly improved. One of the things he discovered was that as some normal vehicles could be protected from small roadside bombs and made bullet proof with armoured plating and bullet proof glass added to them. If the doors or windows of a protected vehicle were open when a bomb went off nearby, then there was every chance that those inside would be killed or seriously injured, even if the armour protected the vehicle itself. Harry got on well with his comrades and initially enjoyed being a member of the Australian SAS and their military training activities.  When he was asked along with his comrades to take part in helping to put a stop to forest fires, he joined in and played his part in trying to put out the fires as expected of him but he was not very pleased to be doing this type of duty. He had joined the SAS he thought to destroy terrorists and other evil types or to rescue people from them, not to waste his military skills and possibly even his life in putting out fires in wild country. Even if it did mean protecting others and saving their property. Consequently, he decided to move to Britain and see what work he could find there to suit his thoughts and feelings of wanting to remove from life, terrorists and those who supported them.  He arrived in London just as they were developing a new secret specialist organisation to remove Known or potential terrorists and their supporters. Harry believed that by joining such an organisation his thoughts and feelings would be fulfilled as he could be secretly assassinating those terrorists living in Britain who could not for legal reasons be locked away i.e. have proofs that would stand up in court. Also, those from abroad who supported them financially and those smuggling arms and explosives to them. Also smugglers of drugs and those of other dangerous and evil behaviour, who some believed, even if imprisoned would when they gained their freedom return to the evil practices of their past. Due to his background which was well known to those involved in the fight against terrorism due to it being talked about by his father's brother IAN who had been a member of MI5 Harry was contacted and after an interview with the person in charge of the new organisation, Sir Cameron Bradley-Stewart, Harry was offered a position in the new organisation with a decent salary. Harry was also contacted by his father's brother who having lost his own brother and sister in law and being a former member of MI5. Offered to help Harry find a suitable house to live privately in. He said he would also find one that had good train contact with London Paddington which would be very useful for Harry as it would enable him to return to London for meetings with his leader, Sir Cameron Bradley-Stewart or to make contact with other members of the organisation in their offices in Baker Street. Harry's uncle found a former large farmhouse to live in, he offered Harry the deposit required to purchase it and helped Harry arrange a mortgage. Once he moved into the house Harry was contacted by his father's brother again. Harry discovered that his father's brother lived nearby just outside the same village and

Knowing Sir Cameron as well as a lot about the new organisation that Harry had joined. His father's brother had helped Harry buy a quiet, high wall surrounded house. In the Oxford part of the Cotswolds near a small lovely and very peaceful village called Kingham, where he could remain secretly and safe once he began his work. A house which Harry was pleased to accept as it was in part of England that not only was very peaceful and out of the way of most big cities but was also very friendly and beautiful, with a post office, a grocers shop and a nice public house and all this helped Harry to settle into the house quickly.

# Chapter Two

Whilst Harry worked for Sir Cameron, by carrying out the removal of Terrorists, Drug smugglers and other evil people, as well as their supporters. In some weeks he wasn't given any tasks to do.

So had quite a bit of free time, sometimes a whole day or even three. Harry as well as running in the hills near where he lived to keep fit. Also practiced his military skills. Such as shooting which he did on a military camp near a not too far away town called Bicester. He also would do a private job for someone else that he knew, especially a friend who had been upset by some evil character. Currently he had agreed to help a friend who lived near him and whose young daughter had been forced to have sex with some paedophile which had ruined her life and really upset her father who was a good friend of Harry and also quite wealthy and had offered Harry some money to carry out the removal of the paedophile. These very rare extra jobs sometimes earned Harry some extra money. He would only do these jobs if it meant he was removing someone who was definitely known to have committed evil activities. He also would only do them if it was safe to do so without it getting in the way of his main occupation. He never did it just to please a friend or because the person had offered him a large sum of money. No matter how close a friend they were and definitely not if it meant he was being asked to remove a non evil person. Harry now was engaged in the removal of the paedophile because of what the evil the man had carried out and the harm he had done to the young girl and also because he could be going to do something similar again to some other young girl. The well-built man and the young woman had entered the hotel room together and the elderly man immediately began to undress himself without having any conversation. The young woman was lit by the bedside lamp, her hair cut short added to her boyish look which in turn added to her appearance of youth, she seemed to be about fourteen or fifteen.

As she stepped across the room her slim narrow hips and tight shorts also added even more to her youth. The watcher recognised her as the prostitute called Laura he had met in Soho and who was now being helpful to him. Doing as he had asked her to do and was paying her to do. She approached the naked man standing in the hotel room and could see he was looking welcoming he was tall well muscled but beginning to let himself go a little, with some thickening of the waist and greying of the hair on his chest. He reached out to the girl pulling her to himself. Pushing her hands against his chest she turned him backwards to the bed and then began kissing and biting one of his nipples causing him to step backwards, his legs now touching the bed

 As she kissed his other nipple there was a soft moan from him and his hands came up off her back to stroke her hair. The hidden watcher felt himself begin to become aroused by the erotic act he was witnessing. Harry Markham masked and hiding behind the curtains that covered the balcony doors was feeling uncomfortable as he watched the girl gently push the man towards the bed, she pushed him down onto the bed and he rolled back lifting his legs off the floor as he lay on the bed the girl straddled him and they began to cuddle with the young woman squeezing and stroking the man, the man's breathing was quickening now and he groaned loudly, stroking along the girl's back. Markham tensed, for his moment was near and he would only have seconds to act when the right moment came. Suddenly the man cried out and arched hisback Markham stepped out from behind the curtains, swiftly crossed the room to the couple on the bed. With one hand he reached out clamped across the man's throat whilst his other hand pushed his small lightly loaded silenced pistol into the man's open mouth. Fired two shots using his very lightly powered bullets designed only to be used over very short distances so as not to make much noise. Again the man's body arched, this time the girl rolled away to rise and stand by the bedside. The body on the bed jerked a few more times before it lay still.

Barely a minute had passed as Markham stood up and looked across at the girl. Saying,"You did well Laura you've earned your money." "and you! enjoyed every minute of it," she said, her tongue flickered across her lips, then she smiled," Markham stepped around the bed and moved towards the young woman. His left hand came out of his pocket And then tossed a roll of banknotes onto the bed saying here is what I promised you. The young woman laughing at his obvious discomfort. Turned to pick them up. As she turned Markham's pistol again appeared in his right hand pointing at her he said, "Laura We need to get out of here as quickly as possible. I know that big git was a paedophile who damaged the lives of a large number of young girls. The police will still consider his death as murder. Come on get ready so you can go out by the way I came in. I hope you aren't afraid of heights ,you have to go down a rope ladder. The young woman began to get ready as quickly as she could putting on a nice, coloured blouse and a pair of tight blue jeans followed by a light blue denim jacket to help keep her warm when she went outside. Meanwhile Harry prepared to leave, he was dressed in a shabby black suit like a waiter would wear and had grown a small moustache for the occasion still hidden by his mask. The moustache together with some fake  slight tan gave him a Mediterranean appearance.  He helped the young woman out onto the balcony, saying to her, A friend of mine will pull up alongside you in his car, enter the car quickly and he will take you to wherever you want to go." Then he directed  her onto the balcony and helped her climb down the ladder and watched her walk down the street until he saw  a car stop beside her.  A man he recognised got out and helped her get into it, what she didn't know was, the man was a colleague of Harrys and worked for the same assassination organisation that Harry worked for and the car had false number plates . Which belonged to a car that was registered in Newcastle and belonged to another member of the assassination organisation who at this time was carrying out a task abroad something which could be proved should the police ask about his car. Now  still parked at Heathrow airport. Harry,s friend unlike what Harry had said to the young woman was going to take her to where Harry wanted her to go which was to Harry's house. A place where Harry could make arrangements with the young woman to enable her to move away and hide someplace where the police couldn't find her and question her about the death of the paedophile. When Laura realised, she was not being taken to where she had asked the driver to take her. She now became very disturbed and frightened. Then when the car stopped for a red traffic light, she tried to open the door to get out only to find it wouldn't open. Probably she thought he has put on the child proof lock to stop me getting out. She now became very frightened indeed and asked the driver why he wasn't taking her to where she had asked him to, which was back to her flat in Soho. The driver immediately produced a small pistol and pointing it at her said I am taking you to Harry's house he wants to arrange for you to move to someplace safe where the police won't find you and question you about what happened today and then probably lock you away in prison. Please Don't panic. Harry just wants to make you safe. This calmed Laura and she became more settled again on her seat in the car.

As soon as Harry had seen the young woman get into his friend's car. Harry removed his mask and let himself out of the room, locking the door behind himself and headed down the stairs, anyone now seeing him would think he was someone who worked in the hotel and hopefully not pay too much attention to him.

Once out in the street he shambled along not appearing to hurry but still covering the ground quite quickly, He now began to consider what he had risked in not killing the young woman to keep himself safe as well as he had killed the paedophile. He had let her go  because she had done so much to help him in the removal of the Paedophile, even if she was a prostitute he had met in Soho. Now he managed to appear as just another hotel worker making his way home. Harry entered the London underground his first destination would be Waterloo because that was where was placed the left luggage lockers you were able to open yourself. It was there he had left a change of clothing. When he arrived there, he collected his change of clothing. Walked about a hundred metres along the footpath outside the station. He had previously scouted the area to make sure there were no street cameras anywhere near. He entered a McDonalds and made his way to the disabled toilet; it was the work of only a few minutes to transfer himself from the shuffling waiter into the country gentleman. Gone was the moustache and the fake tan was washed off, the black suit had been replaced by an expensive tweed jacket and corduroy trousers, the polished cheap black slip-on shoes replaced with a pair of brown brogues from Lobbs and Co. St James' street London, even the bag when turned inside out was to reveal an expensive leather look. Standing tall, it was a well-dressed country gentleman carrying an expensive looking leather bag who left the restaurant. Harry now walked quickly the short distance across Westminster bridge and into the underground, this time his destination was Paddington, he was on his way home. Robert Markham, once an orphan, a Rhodesian Selous scout and sometime later a member of the Australian S.A.S. was now Harry Markham a country gentleman. Who lived in a large house with a large garden and a long drive up to a parking area by its front steps and door. All of this surrounded by a ten foot high wall which insured Harry's privacy. The house was a converted farmhouse on the outskirts of the quiet Cotswold village called Kingham. Arriving at Paddington he boarded the Thames train that was to take him to Charlbury where he had left his car parked, not in the station carpark where it would be too noticeable being left all day but in the middle of the village near a housing estate where if he was delayed no one would really notice it. The ten-minute walk to his car gave him a chance to relax and let down his guard a little bit, He quickly went through the operation he had just committed in London as he strolled along, analysing each part looking for a mistake that could lead back to him. He felt good about this one, he had been paid a lot of money to remove a monster who preyed on young girls and for once he felt a satisfaction that came not just from the money he had earned but from the safety he had created for others less capable of dealing with such a monster. As regards Laura, Harry was expecting to meet her again when the colleague he had arranged to collect her and bring her to his house and meet him, arrived. This was to be when the evening became dark so that Harry could allow her into his house without anyone else knowing and send her away to somewhere that the police wouldn't find her and also where she could have a reasonable life. Soon after entering his home Harry was expecting in a short time to be joined by his colleague Frank with Laura. His friendly colleague had been chosen specially by Harry to help him get Laura to his house as this friend would also be able to help Harry to send her away to some place safe. His friendly colleague called Franky Norman was from Northern Ireland and had lived in a seaside resort there, called Bangor, where he had worked building large sailing yachts and had sailed them several times to

Scotland and back, He had also been a member of the B specials an auxiliary police force used to support the police on a regular basis as well as help defend against the IRA. and had lost a number of his relations when a bomb attack was made by terrorists on a bus. Hence his reason for joining the assassination organisation was similar to that of Harry. Franky had agreed to help Harry move Laura to Bangor where he said he would find her a council flat to live in, on an estate close to the town in a very quiet, attractive area to live in and he would also find her a good job to do in the nearby famous Holiday town of Bangor.

Thanks to the advice and help of Sir Cameron, Harry had obtained a Dakota C47 plane which he kept at a private airfield near where he lived and where Sir Cameron had arranged things so that Harry who had learned to fly while living in Australia, could take off and land there without anyone querying what he was doing. He could therefore bring from his work for the anti terrorist organisation, the dead bodies of those he had killed and that he would in future want to dispose of secretly, to this plane and drop them far out over the Atlantic. In an area where they would hopefully be eaten before ever being washed ashore on any beach off the west coast of Ireland which was the part of the islands of Great Britain and Ireland nearest to the Atlantic Ocean. He was going to take Franky and Laura to Newtownards private airfield in Northern Ireland in a few days' time early one morning, because Newtownards was not far from Bangor and then let them carry on with their arrangements from there. He was also going to give Laura the rest of the cash he had been given for removing the paedophile and so help to persuade her to go with Franky and have a good start. The drive home would take him about 15 minutes and he looked forward to meeting with Franky and discussing with him and Laura their journey to northern Ireland when they arrived at his house. Then when he had discussed things with them and persuaded Laura to go with

Franky, he could have a long soak in the bath a change of clothes, then  make an enjoyable meal for the three of them and provide a nice glass of wine each for Franky and Laura and for himself a glass or two of Taliskar Scotch whiskey with a little water added, a drink for which he had developed a loving taste, Perhaps a drink he had begun to drink in memory of his father who had enjoyed it very much but Harry always dismissed this, there was no room for sentimentality in his life or worry or even love. There had been some women in his life since leaving Rhodesia. Some relationships had lasted a few weeks, one or two even a month, but something always spoiled it because on Harry's part there was never any love, sometimes there was convenience, or sex, or friendship but never love and so nothing lasted. Sitting in his comfortable living room, Harry Markham having showered, relaxed, then wined and dined while waiting for Franky and Laura was watching late night news on television because he wanted the weather forecast for the next few days as he intended to fly Franky and Laura to Northern Ireland and then when he returned home, go for a long walk in the Malvern's and enjoy a pub lunch. After which  he would have to once again report to Sir Cameron and probably have to prepare for another assassination attempt. His thoughts were on which route he would take when having his walk, when these thoughts were interrupted by the phone ringing, at first he chose to ignore it, he was ex-directory and few of his friends who had his telephone number would call him at this hour. Then he realised it was the phone in his study, he groaned and rose to answer it, knowing in his heart there would be no walk in the Malvern's tomorrow. He picked up the phone in his study making sure the scrambler was switched

on.

"At last! I've been trying to get hold of you all day," a high pitched somewhat feminine voice said, "Sir Cameron wants to see you at once." Harry said in reply, "calm down Freddie, you'll only give yourself ulcers, tell me what's going on that can't wait until tomorrow". Freddie again spoke saying, "I don't know exactly, only the boss wants to see you, he's got an important job for you, something to do with smuggling, possibly arms and explosives or even  drugs, they are  being smuggled by three British men using a very special yacht moored at Eastbourne in Sussex . that they sail from there to somewhere  in North Africa by way of the Mediterranean sea, where they collect the things they are smuggling back into England.

 The honourable Freddy Brannigan, son of an obscure Irish baronet was the secretary to Sir Cameron Bradley- Stuart, who was in charge of the organisation Harry now worked for, Freddy was gay, very camp, almost a caricature of gayness and also the finest pistol shot Harry Markham had ever known.

"OK OK stay calm, I'm not going anywhere tonight, so let me talk to Sir Cameron". There was a squeak on the line and a different voice, brusque, hoarse and authoritive, said, "I want you here and want you here fast Markham. Make sure you're in my office as early tomorrow as you can, I know you and Frank Norman have been up to mischief over the last couple of days you've had free. Franky can continue to stay wherever he wants to as he is on his holiday break for this year and he still has quite a few more free days before he should be back at work. But I need you here, so I can explain to you the next job I want you to do, I need you here as soon as possible because you'll need to think of a plan and I'll have to pass the information you give me to the colleagues you'll ask me to appoint to help you carry it out. While they are still free to help you and don't have other tasks to do, that I have given them." Harry replied "I fully understand your hurry however I need to ask you to do something for me so I can get to you as early tomorrow as you need me and still sort out a problem which I will tell you about when we meet tomorrow  again, Please when I give you a little of the details of what help I need.. Could you make a flight plan for me and get me permission to fly my plane from it's present base to Newtownards private airfield in Northern Ireland as I need to take Franky and a young woman to it the day after tomorrow, early in the morning. They have both been helping me and now I must enable them to make some arrangements to keep the young woman safe from police here in England as she knows what I have been up to earlier today. Which was the removal of a very cruel paedophile who has been in prison and had been let out early and could have continued with his horrible behaviour which ruined the life of the daughter of a friend of mine who I trusted very much and had discussed with me what my job was and consequently asked me to remove the evil paedophile permanently and offered me some money to  help me do it. I know you can and hope you will make the flight plan and get it accepted for me, it's very late tonight but you should be able to do it tomorrow as I want to leave early in the morning of the day after tomorrow.  Then  I'll be able to see you  tomorrow, early in the morning and tell you all about what my problem is as well as providing you with a plan to sort out what you are wanting me to do about the yacht owners you believe to be smuggling something dangerous into the country. When I will be able to hear exactly what the action is that you have chosen for me to carry out and listened to calmly by me so that I will understand exactly what is expected. I should be able to make a suitable plan, Goodbye now see you tomorrow early, I must let you go now so that I can try to have a good night's sleep." With that Harry put the phone down and went and had another drink, before he undressed and prepared himself for bed. Intending to have an early night and get up very early in the morning to go and see Sir Cameron as early in the day as possible.  There   was a knock on his front door which he hoped would be his very friendly colleague Frank with the young woman helper from the paedophile killing in London, so he went to the door and opened it to see Frank and the girl standing there. He invited them in with a smile on his face and the girl said why has this man brought me here instead of to my own home? Harry replied you told me you were still under pressure and worried about what we did earlier today and wanted me to try and relieve you.  Now you have your chance, come on in and sit down and have a cup of tea while I send Frank away to bed and we can talk about what we can do in the comfort  and safety of this house. Come and sit down on the sofa with me and enjoy a nice cup of tea and a slice of bread and ham, then we can go upstairs together and see if you can earn another good sum of money. The girl smiled again and said, "yes of course I will, with pleasure." Finishing their drinks and enjoying a small bite to eat they went upstairs the girl going first and as she reached the top Harry took out his silenced pistol.  Then took her back down stairs and further down to his cellar where he was going to make her the offer and said to Laura, "either have  an  other £800 and go with Frank to find a place to live in and a good job to do or be shot now, here in the cellar. I want to make sure you aren't arrested by the police and possibly tell them about me so either I remove you completely with this pistol or help Frank to move you to a nice place and set you up comfortably and with all that you need, in a place where the police won't find you. "Laura answered with a question, "where is Frank going to take me and help me to live and get a good job?" Harry replied "He came from Northern Ireland originally and I am going to fly you both there, in  the morning after tomorrow and give you another 800 pounds. So you should have sixteen hundred pounds to give you a start and Frank will stay with you and help you find a nice flat near where he used to live which is a very well known and popular holiday centre by the sea . He will also introduce you to some of his past friends that also live there, They will offer you a pleasant job, Frank will also help you to get settled by helping you to meet many of his former friends and they will offer you friendship and company as well, they won't know anything about your naughty past which you won't need to carry out any more to make a decent living. Laura liked what she was hearing and with a smile said, "yes please." Harry now asked Frank to take her back up to the lounge and before they went up gave her the second eight hundred pounds, then followed them up, had another drink of whiskey while Laura and Frank each enjoyed a glass of wine and then Harry took her upstairs to his bedroom where he had a second single bed as well as his double that he liked to sleep in and directed her to sleep in the single bed. Harry then locked the bedroom door and went down to his office where he rang Sir Cameron to check if the flight plan had been accepted yet and was told that it was too late at night to be doing the setting up of a flight plan but that it could be done in the morning without any problems and how he should be able to go to go to Newtonards the following morning as he had planned. Now ready to have his sleep, Harry returned upstairs again to his bedroom in which Laura had settled on the single bed and was fast asleep. Harry set his alarm to Wake him at six am. so that he could have his usual  nice traditional English breakfast of two fried eggs a piece of fried bacon and some fried tomatoes with a couple of slices of toast all of which this time he would have to increase in quantity and share with Frank and Laura, Then when they had finished enjoying their breakfast and after getting ready quickly, Harry would drive  to the nearest rail station and go and visit Sir Cameron, Telling Frank and Laura that he would come back in good time to take them to the nearby private airfield where he kept his Dakota aircraft,   and help them to board it, he explained to them how the evening before he had contacted Sir Cameron and asked him to arrange a flight plan to enable him to fly to the

Newtonards airfield so that he could take off first thing in the morning of the following day. So that he could get back to London this morning in time for him to see Sir Cameron to make the arrangements for his next task. Later that same morning Harry arrived at Sir Cameron's office and again asked if he had completed the flight plan and had it accepted and was told yes indeed. Now he expected to be able to explain to Sir Cameron what he had been up to the previous day and what his problem was. Then he expected to find out what was the new task Sir Cameron wanted Him to deal with and which colleagues he was going to work with, Sir Cameron had agreed to do the flight plan for the next day and had got it accepted, so that Harry would be free to arrive at the meeting with him early this morning and have enough time to think out the plan that Harry thought best to enable the his new task of sorting out the smugglers to be carried out properly and to discover how Harry's plan to deal with the problem would need to be organised, so that he could pass it on to any other members of the organisation that would be required to support Harry in completing it. This was to enable them to get involved in planning what to do to help   Harry, Before they had become engaged in other tasks and events, possibly not set up by Sir Cameron.

# Chapter Three

arriving early in the assassin organisations offices, the morning after he had removed the paedophile, Harry Markham chatted to Sir Cameron about his problem with the possibility of Laura being spoken to by the police and how he had dealt with it. Harry Now stood in front of Sir Cameron's large oak desk, like some naughty schoolboy about to receive a telling off by his headmaster. Harry had a small problem with his job which was that Sir Cameron Chose people with not only an attitude and proof of no difficult feelings about killing those who were responsible for evil. Sir Cameron also checked that those he wished to employ were already skilled and fit enough to carry out the tasks he required of them. The Little problem for Harry as well as for some of his colleagues was that Unfortunately the organisation did no fitness training or any other military training of it's members as it didn't have a camp ground similar to that of the army or that of the police. Instead the members were left to look after themselves in their free time during the gaps between the organisation's tasks required of them by Sir Cameron, they were therefore expected to carry out their own training. Keeping fit by going for runs or long marches on hills in their free time and perhaps joining shooting clubs where they could practice their shooting and keep their standards high. They were also encouraged to join Martial arts sports clubs such as karate or Kungfu, to also use in their spare time and so develop their unarmed attack or self defence ability. Harry as a result had joined a Kungfu club and using his TRAPS identity card had also become a member of a military run rifle shooting club as well as a pistol shooting club at the same camp. Close to a town called Bicester not too far from where he lived and as a result had maintained his ability in the use of these weapons. He also did a lot of walking and running in the hills near where he lived and also carried out some killings of evil people, he knew about.

Who had not been set up by Sir Cameron. So long as Harry knew as true fact that he was definitely either saving lives or preventing lives being ruined by evil,  such as terrorism, drug supplying, or paedophiles as in his recent action, he was very happy to carry out his own killings with the help of his colleague friends from the TRAPS. organisation.

"You absent yourself without telling anyone, you go walk about for days, then you're on some sort of private job, don't we pay you enough?" said an angry Sir Cameron, then he threw a copy of the Times newspaper at Markham and said again angrily, "was this you? It's got all your hall marks. Some wicked forty-year-old paedophile released early from prison who had been given life for committing sex with a number of underage girls, ruined their lives and was still young enough to possibly want to continue with his fowl law breaking, His release was not approved by the parents of his victims who had written letters of complaint to various newspapers. According to that newspaper I tossed to you just now. He ended up dead while naked, in a hotel room in London. Shot through the mouth, the killer is now being hunted by the police. Carry on like this and you could find yourself out of a job." Not that that will bother you but it will if you end up in prison yourself. I would have to sack you and nobody else would hire you, the trouble with you Markham, is your so bloody good at what you do and you know it and what's worse I know it too, dam you". Harry waited for the tirade to end, it always did, usually with the arrival of Freddie Brannigan and a tray on which was a pot of Earl Grey tea and a plate of biscuits. Then he initially denied part of the accusation by Sir Cameron saying," I am earning enough from you and find the work I do for you is too important for me to risk losing it by doing things you wouldn't approve of,  I have been spending my days walking and running in the Malvern hills near where I live, to keep myself fit and yes I did remove a wicked Paedophile yesterday  not because I was paid lots of money  but because he was an evil man who had damaged the lives of lots of young girls and might continue to do it again. Surely that's something you should be pleased about as he was very evil."  If Freddie Brannigan was a caricature of everything camp, then Sir Cameron was a caricature of everything British Home office and Spies. A curious mixture of yes minister and James Bond.

Within this caricature was a keen brain with superb organisational qualities, that had first drawn him to a prime minister's attention, and had kept him in the leadership position that Sir Cameron had remained in ever since he was  made head of the Committee for studies of terrorism and it's causes, so that imprisoned terrorists or known potential terrorists could be treated psychologically and persuaded to change their way of thinking, an obscure quango with a budget that far outweighed anything it's title might indicate that it deserved. Over the years he had been encouraged to change the committee to become a more aggressive organisation known as "Terrorist raider assassination provider selection" or TRAPS. for short.  Involving specially chosen and skilled assassins and technicians. People capable of removing terrorists from abroad or people from the U. K. who were known to be terrorists or those that encouraged terrorism or other forms of evil such as drug or weapon importing and supplying. Without sufficient proof to have them proven guilty in court and sent to prison or the removal of those imprisoned and then released yet still capable of committing terrorism or other evil crimes. The original committee had been set up on the instructions of the Heath government in 1972 following the hijacking of planes and the subsequent British loss of face when the government caved in and some terrorists were released following the destruction of the planes at Dawson's field airport in Jordon. Currently the quango still maintained it's original title in public, "Committee for the study of terrorism and it's causes", so that no one would know about and object to it's aggressive activities. Calming down Sir Cameron said, "I now have a very important job for you which I believe will suit your cleaver planning as well as your anti-terrorist character."

" Now Harry please  listen carefully." Said Sir Cameron. After a short pause, In which he had poured two cups of tea."I have had a report about some boat owners who appear to be bringing something evil from north Africa, possibly drugs or guns and explosives, but the Police have searched the boat and haven't been able to find anything or any proper evidence of anything. So they have passed it on to us to try and sort out, if we get any proof of importing weapons or explosives then perhaps the boat could blow up whilst at sea was the suggestion". Next he said,"The police not only searched the boat but also had sniffer dogs on it, some which would have smelt any drugs and others who would have smelt any explosives or ammunition, so we really have a problem in trying to find out the truth. However I have already carried out some enquiries and discovered that they take a scuba diver with them each time they go, so I thought we might try and replace him with you as I know it is one of the sports you have indulged in since leaving Rhodesia. How you come about joining them I leave up to you but if you need any help with your plan let me know and I will do what I can, OK now let's have a cup of tea while you think about your plan and then you can leave and finalise what you think you might do." Harry nodded and sat down to enjoy the Tray of tea and biscuits Freddie Brannigan had brought in. After a little time, Harry asked, "where is the boat based?" Sir Cameron answered, "at Eastbourne Marina,"

"Right," said Harry, "let me have a few hours to think of a plan. " After three hours of peaceful thinking in the organisation's library office about what he would have to do to join the crew of the boat and the study of maps and other information about the area  where the  boat was moored near, that he was able to read about in books. Harry was able to approach Sir Cameron with his plan, which he told to Sir Cameron. He said, "First remove their scuba diver, either get the police to arrest him or better, use members of our team to kidnap him and keep him for 6 months or longer as secretly and quietly as possible. Do this just before they are next about to leave for a trip and keep him for as long as necessary until I have finished with the rogues.   As part of my plan to join them I'll be lying in a rubber dinghy in the water off the shore of Seaford or Seahaven as the boat is passing by and will fire a help flare into the air and hope they will stop and save me. I will be in my scuba gear and will tell them that my friends and I were planning scuba diving looking for wrecks as we had heard there were quite a few off that part of the coast also that just as I was about to make my dive our boat had been driven into by a ferry vessel returning to Seahaven from France and our boat began to sink quickly but unfortunately for me as I tried to remove my oxygen tanks and mask. My friends were able to board a dinghy with a motor and get away while I was stuck with this one, without a motor or paddles or any means of driving it anywhere and it was being drawn out to sea by the tide and the currents so I was panicking as my so called friends had abandoned me and I could end up having to try and swim back to the shore which in spite of my ability to swim well and wearing my diving suit to help keep me warm would have been very difficult. I might well have drowned. I shall still be wearing my scuba wet suit and I hope they will offer me the job of replacement for their missing diver which after a hesitation I will let them persuade me to do," then I will go with them to North Africa probably via the Mediterranean and will learn what their plan is and how they are fooling the police searches." Sir Cameron agreed with the plan but said I think the timing will have to be very exact, you will need to know the exact time they leave Eastbourne so you can get ready and wait for them without putting yourself in too much danger and yet be ready on the water and also in the right position for them to see your signal for help and be not too far from you We will have to get an accurate definition of their exact route along the east Sussex coast. I will ring the local coast guards and see what information I can find out about the situation. After a little time having made Phone calls to the coast guards in the area and finding out what he thought Harry needed to know to carry out his plan successfully. Sir Cameron said to Harry. "The whole thing will have to coincide with a ferry crossing from France which means in daytime it will have to be about 9:00am, or if afternoon or evening 3:30pm 5:30pm 9:00pm 11:00pm so afternoon or night time looks like our best chance, next I will check out what time they normally leave and get back to you". A few hours later Sir Cameron had carried out his research with the police as to what time the boat usually left East Bourne and to find that the route usually taken by the boat was about three miles out from the Sussex coast and the normal leaving time was usually between 8:00pm and 9:00pm so if you get ready for the evening they will be leaving when we know what time that will be, then all should fit nicely. At this point Sir Cameron Told Harry to prepare for his work and settle at his home and await a telephone call from him with the final details. Which Harry agreed to and said he would be ready for the call. He then returned home to his house near Kingham and prepared his scuba wet suit and flippers so he could wear them when called on the day of his job. He also had to think wither or not he would have a plan to kill all the members of the boat while they were in the Mediterranean or closer to Britain or just tell the police what they had been smuggling into the country and how. Harry made his decision about this when he was told that there would be at least three others on the boat and they would possibly all be armed, whereas he would at best have just a diving knife if even that, He would let the police deal with the problem and if required he would remove the men later, on land.

Eventually with the boat leaving at a suitable time Harry was able to carry out his plan to be left floating in his wet suit and some other parts of his scuba kit, several miles from the shore in a rubber dinghy without any means of driving it towards the shore and seeing the yacht coming in the distance he waited for it to get closer to him and fired his rescue flare and was rescued by the boat as expected. On board the boat he overheard a conversation between two of the men about wither they should have bothered to rescue him or not, one of whom said it was a normal and proper thing to do at sea while the other argued against it and said it would affect their trip, the other one now said we have gained another scuba diver by being proper seamen and picking up a person in danger. Next Harry was asked to join the group and do some scuba diving for them. Which after a hesitation and the appearance of  thinking about it on his part, he was offered a large sum of money to help, which he agreed to. Throughout the journey the men began to talk to Harry and ask him about his past which he told them a little truth about, such as his education at a school in South Africa and his leaving Rhodesia when the government changed then lied saying his family were becoming frightened and went to live in Australia where he had learned to do his scuba diving but after a time began to become fed up with things and came back to Britain to live with his uncle who was his father's brother and had been born in England and had remained in Britain when Harry's own father  had left to go with Harry's grandfather who was his uncles father and who owned a farm that Harry's father was given in the will when his father Died in what was then known as southern Rhodesia. Harry told them he now enjoyed living in England with his uncle who he said worked as a teacher in a private school where he lived and enabled Harry to continue with his hobbies of fencing and scuba diving by getting Harry a job working as a gardener and sports field mower in the same school which gave Harry sufficient free time to do his hobbies. Apart from a bit of a storm as they crossed the Bay of Biscay the boat journey was quite pleasant and Harry enjoyed it as he was able to stay very relaxed even though he had no experience of long boat trips in a motor yacht.

Once near Algiers off the North African coast. He was asked to get ready to enter the water and did so, then the boat arrived at a buoy floating in the water and Harry was told the boat had an underwater door in the keel

When you go down you will find hanging from the buoy a number of plastic bags to keep things dry, open the door in the keel and place the bags neatly in the underwater hold please. Before making the dive Harry asked the men, "what would you have done if you hadn't found me?" One of the men answered, "WE would have pulled the buoy onto the boat and dragged the bags back through the water which would have been fine so long as there wasn't any storms such as the one we had as we crossed the Bay of Biscay.  In which case we could have lost them all". Having made the dive and Holding the bags and squeezing them as he put them in the  hold Harry realised that several of them contained pistols and two other larger bags contained what felt like rifles while some felt like they had something soft in them which could have been plastic explosives and several others had metal boxes, which Harry thought could contain ammunition and three bags had just one hard box which Harry thought probably contained drugs to add to their profits, So the smugglers were bringing weapons into the country as well as drugs and of course the police dogs could smell nothing as nothing had entered the boat proper and all  had been carried under the water, so when the boat was stopped and searched there was nothing to be found as there was no on board opening to the underwater hold.

On the way back Harry was warned by the three men that he would be killed if he told anyone about what they had done, Harry replied why would I tell anyone when you are smuggling something, possibly drugs and are offering to give me a large sum of money and could possibly take me on a number of other times as well, all to my benefit. This calmed the three men who smiled, and one said it will take a couple of weeks for us to give you your money as we will have to sell the stuff first OK? Fine said Harry don't worry about me I will come and meet you where you keep the boat. Harry had suddenly arrived at a plan on how to remove the smugglers he thought if they are going to take me on some of their next trips, I will be able to bring my pistol with me, in my bag amongst my diving equipment and deal with all three as we cross the bay of Biscay or while we are still in the Mediterranean, At this point one of the men asked Harry where he lived and he gave them the address of the private school in the Cotswolds where his uncle worked that Harry also lived in and where he worked. Oh! Said the man, "what made you come this far to do scuba diving". Harry replied, "only the possibility of finding a wreck that was very valuable and it was the choice of those so called friends who let me down and had previously convinced me that they knew what they were doing, if you would like me to join you for your next trip I think I'll find a place to stay in Eastbourne". "Good idea," said the man, "if you do manage it, pop your contact details on the boat as it will be moored in Eastbourne marina where we will dive under ourselves with snorkels and give the contents directly to our customers who know roughly when we will arrive back and come to meet us and  to take away the goods  before the police come again to check us, that way we create no evidence for the police to use, Then we will contact you, even if our other diver turns up again, you did a quicker and better job than he normally did". Once on the shore Harry contacted Sir Cameron as quickly as possible and told him of his new plan and asked him not to tell the police about the smuggling boat and it's secret under water hold but to try and have some members of Sir Cameron's team to prepare to spy on the next trip and also spy on the three smugglers arrival back and try to find out who they were giving the weapons to at the marina and where the customers were taking the weapons to. So that when he returned from his third trip with the smugglers, he could also find and remove the customers who must be terrorists preparing to carry out some attack My colleagues must keep a watch on them in case they try to carry out their attack before I can remove them. Sir Cameron agreed to the new plan and said he would do as Harry asked. Harry found himself a flat to live in at Eastbourne and left a message on the boat with the address on it and saying he would be pleased to help with the next trip. Two weeks later Harry received a message from the boat owners. Telling him the next trip would be in a fortnights time on the first Wednesday of the month at approximately 8:00pm and he should also get ready, it also contained £500 cash and a note of thanks for his previous help and a warning that he would be welcome to join them again for a third trip on the third Wednesday of the next month. Two weeks later Harry was ready to go again but not yet ready to remove the smugglers as he wanted his colleagues to find out about the customers who he also wanted to remove as they were probably the actual killer terrorists. Two weeks later on the Wednesday at 8:00pm Harry was ready to go he brought a bag containing his diving equipment He Joined the three smugglers on their boat in Eastbourne he then said, "thank you very much for the cash and also for telling me the date of your next trip I should be pleased to join you again on it," he was welcomed and they went off in their usual direction heading for the Mediterranean. Harry was made very welcome by the three men and thanked them very much for the cash award he had received. When they arrived at the `Mediterranean and approached the Buoy, Harry began to get his kit ready and put on his wet suit and carried his flippers and mask with him onto the deck. Then when they arrived at the buoy he was helped to place the gas bottles on to his back and to prepare for his dive, which he carried out as before and again realised that what he was loading were bags of guns and possibly explosives and ammunition as well as drugs. Then when he had placed them in the secret hold he boarded the boat and got ready for the journey back. Again he was treated in a very thankful and pleasant manner all the way back to Eastbourne, where he hoped to leave the boat and the three men behind as they were waiting for their customers to arrive and collect their goods however this time the three men asked him to help them get the bags out of the underwater hold and have them ready for when the buyers arrived and then they could just hand them to them. Soon the two customers arrived and Harry still swimming in the water but with his mask off passed the bags up to them on the jetty so they could carry them to their car. Seeing him they now knew Harry was one of the smugglers.

A few days later Sir Cameron was again talking to Harry and Harry explained to him that he intended to take the two buyers to a beach hut at Seaford and there shoot them and then get rid of them, could Sir Cameron rent one of the beach huts there from the council owners

And let Harry know which one it was. Also could he arrange for three of his colleagues to be ready with a small motor boat to come out from Seaford beach when he arrived off the coast there in the smuggler's boat and take the goods to the beach hut and get ready for when Harry brought the buyers there and also be ready to shoot the two men as soon as they entered the hut, using silenced pistols. Sir Cameron agreed with this plan and just as Harry was setting off for his third trip told him it was all arranged, so he could carry out his plan. The third time Harry went with the smugglers to fetch more weapons he had his pistol hidden amongst his diving kit.

As they crossed the Mediterranean and approached the buoy as before, Harry began to prepare his scuba kit and armed himself with his pistol then quickly went on deck and shot each of the men in the head before any of them could do anything to stop him. He then threw them overboard and took control of the boat and before turning it around and heading back towards Britain, he pulled the buoy and the contents of the bags tied to it on to the boat then turned the boat around and began heading back the way they had come hoping he would be able to manage it safely back to Eastbourne as driving a boat was not one of the things he had had any practice at. He was very lucky as the weather was good and the steering of the boat easy to carry out with a large compass nearby and easy to see that he was heading northwest until he saw the coastof Spain in front and then turning towards the west and following the coast towards Gibraltar, After this things got more difficult as he didn't know exactly which direction to go in after passing Gibraltar, he guessed he should continue a little further out towards the west into the Atlantic and then head north with the coast of Portugal in view until he arrived at the bay of Biscay and after passing across the Bay of Biscay he arrived at the coast of France at the northern end of the bay which he recognised having seen it five times previously on the first and second trip and the first part of this journey. Then arriving at the Northern end of the Bay he continued around the coast and continued north until he spotted the coast of England There were a number of charts in the steering cabin and Harry studied those he thought applied to the area of English coast which he was hoping to approach and thought if he carried on along until he was opposite Seaford. Which he expected to recognise as he had seen it as well as other parts of the coast, several times before, on the other boat trips he had made with the smugglers. There he would be met by His colleagues in a small boat who would take the bags of weapons and drugs to the rented beach hut as he had requested Sir Cameron to arrange. When the two buyers arrived to meet him when he arrived at Eastbourne marina, he told them the importers had asked him to tell the buyers that they were trying a new method to pass on the weapons because the police had been pestering them before they set off to fetch the new load. He then told them that because of the police constantly searching the boat the collection of goods had been placed in a beach hut at Seaford which was a little way from Eastbourne and the boat had stopped briefly a distance from the beach and the weapons and drugs had been brought ashore in a small out board powered dinghy that would not have aroused any suspicion from anyone as it was only a boat that people would use close to the shore, usually to tow water skiers with. He also told the buyers they could collect the imports from the beach hut, the sooner the better. He asked them when they would come with him to collect the things from the other smugglers who were waiting there for them and said if they followed him as he drove his car he would help them find the beach hut by meeting them by the seated beach shelter on the promenade close to the car parking spaces and taking them to the beach hut which was on it's own near the Martello tower. What he didn't tell them was that he intended to shoot them in the beach hut with a silenced pistol and then drop their bodies from a plane into the Atlantic. The two buyers agreed to meet him there and bring the money to pay the others at the same time. Harry said thank you and I'll meet you at the shelter it is the only one and easy to see on the promenade so it should be easy for us to meet there,   About an hour later, Harry and the three buyers had arrived  and parked near the shelter,  after a few moments Harry and the three buyers had walked along the promenade to the beach hut where two of Harry's colleagues waited their pistols at the ready and with orders to use them immediately on any one brought in by Harry, hopefully with Harry behind them, this was in case he couldn't cope with the two buyers on his own when they entered the beach hut and didn't see any of the other three transporters of the weapons, they might turn on Harry out of suspicion. Arriving with them at the beach hut Harry then unlocked the door and allowed them to enter first, taking out his pistol as he followed them in. Then he heard two quiet shots and each of the two buyers yelled and fell to the floor a bullet wound in each of their heads and two of his three helpers were waiting each side of the doorway a silenced pistol in their hand.  a bag from the boat in one of his hands and a smile on his face the other one was standing at the back of the hut the smuggled bags of weapons lying at his feet causing the two buyers to enter and look down at the floor or up at him not noticing the other two men. Fortunately the beach by this time was not at all crowded with only a few people walking along on the stony beach and looking out to sea and no one walking along the promenade by the beach huts.

Thank you said Harry very well done, all we have to do now is wait until dark and move them to the boot of my car without being seen, then we can take them to my plane to get rid of the bodies in the Atlantic, I will need one of you to fly with me and do the chucking out while I am still flying. So decide now who that will be while we wait for darkness. In the meantime let us go for a gentle walk along the promenade, it has been a lovely sunny day and we should enjoy it. Harry and his three supporters locked the hut door and walked along the promenade and parts of the beach most of the way to Newhaven looking at the very peaceful sea and commenting on what they thought was the vague view of the French coast in the distance. Then they walked back again and arrived at the beach hut just before darkness was falling. A visit to the town of Seaford and a drink in a pub until full darkness was their next act and then the supporters returned to the beach hut while Harry moved his car as close to it as possible. Then checking that no people were about they moved the three dead men into the back of the car partly in the boot and partly on the lowered back seats they covered them with a duvet taken from the beach hut. Harry and the man Kevin who was the one who choose to help him on the plane, drove off on a very long Journey to the Cotswolds and possibly to the private airfield where Harry kept his plane, to place the bodies on the plane so that on another occasion they could fly the plane over the Atlantic and dispose of the bodies. While the other two colleagues travelled to their homes in their own car. Harry and Kevin arrived in the Cotswolds some four hours later and Harry said we'll pop into my house until tomorrow as the private airfield won't be open at this time of night to enable me to make a flight plan. You can enjoy a cup of tea with me or a couple of glasses of wine whichever you prefer and maybe a little to eat as well. "That's a great Idea", said Kevin, "do you have a spare bed for me to use". "Yes indeed," said Harry, "I'll show it to you when we arrive and after you have a drink and a bite to eat you can go off to it until the morning".

Arriving at His house Harry parked the car in the garden then went and opened the garage on one side of the house and parked the car in it to make sure no one could look into the car at any stage and see the bodies, then he opened the house and he and Kevin went in. Harry opened a bottle of white French wine and left it with a couple of glasses on a coffee table by the sofa in the lounge then went into the kitchen after asking Kevin if he would like some scrambled eggs and toast which he said would not take long to prepare. Kevin said, "yes please I do like that as a snack" ten minutes later Harry brought two plates on a tray with two slices of toast and scrambled egg on each plate one for himself and one for Kevin he had managed so quickly by making the scrambled egg in a microwave oven. Kevin joined Harry on the sofa and started eating the meal with the knife and fork that was with it as well as having a drink of wine from time to time. After a few more minutes Harry had finished his food and asked Kevin if he would like a cup of tea which, Kevin answered with, "no thank you I'll just have another glass of this delicious wine it will help me sleep better". Not having shown Kevin His bedroom when they entered the house as soon as Kevin had finished his meal and second glass of wine. Harry asked him to follow him and led the way up the stairs to the first floor where the bedrooms were situated and showed Kevin to a room with an on suite bathroom.

Harry said, "Here is your bedroom, have a shower if you want one, on the bed you will find a towel together with a new tooth brush and tooth paste to use as well as a fresh set of pyjamas to wear in bed. Good night! I'll call you at about 9;00am for breakfast and we will go to the plane later in the day just before dark so that when we get to the plane it will be dark and difficult for anyone to see what we are loading into it and then together we can get rid of the rubbish the next day when it is light and I can create a flight plan, then we come back to my home Where we can get in touch by phone with Sir Cameron and we can spend another night together. In which you will be very welcome. The next day we can return to the plane and take off in daylight after I have given the flight plan and drop the rubbish in the Atlantic. You can ask me to drop you off after we have landed and on the way back towards my home, at a railway station from which trains that run to London stop at and you can make your way to your own home from there or if you would be happy to spend another night with me I will take you home and the next day drop you off in London. Or at your home which ever you feel is best.

Next morning Harry and his helper Kevin enjoyed a nice full English breakfast together. Then went to Harry's car and made sure the three bodies were properly covered and hidden. They next went back in were Harry collected his paperwork which made it easy for him to enter the private airfield without his car being searched as other cars sometimes were. Then they set off to board Harry's Dakota and get rid of the bodies. After about a half hour they arrived at the entrance to the private airfield and Harry opened the car window and showed his special entrance papers to the man on duty at the entrance and then drove to near the landing ground and to his plane.

Together they quickly loaded the three bodies onto the plane first making sure no one was around to see them, then they left the plane and Harry returned to his home again stopping at an Indian restaurant to buy a delicious take away to enjoy that evening.  Next day they awoke at about 8:00am. Had a full English breakfast again of eggs, bacon, fried tomatoes, and bread, then again went to the private airfield this time early in the day so that it would be light for their take off and landing. They immediately boarded the plane, then Harry took his usual route to end up well out over the Atlantic. And Kevin opened the side door of the plane and tossed the bodies out then Harry flew back to the private airfield and as Kevin had chosen to do Harry took him in his car to a nearby railway station at the village of Moreton on the Marsh, to enable Kevin to return to London and visit Sir Cameron as Kevin wished to do, before returning to his own home.

Next morning Harry had taken an early train in order to return to the offices from where he worked and had been sent for by his leader Sir Cameron. Who had rung him to tell him he was needed for a special task to help remove a terrorist camp so as to keep the population safe. Harry having travelled by train from where he lived in the lovely oxford village of Kingham and arrived in London at Paddington station where he usually walked down to the underground to travel to the offices where he worked from and which were in Baker street, decided that as he was early and had some free time would have a walk through a part of London so he could see it as he hadn't seen much of it. He set out to walk up the narrow road that led away from the station. Walking up this road he suddenly noticed two men pulling large knives out of their coats and running toward other people leaving the station to try and stab them. Fortunately for the others, an old man attacked the two men with his walking stick as they ran past him.

One of the two had what looked like a manchete and smashed the stick with it. Harry seeing what was going on quickly took out his pistol and ran towards the old man, shooting the knife man as soon as he was close enough and able to fire up through the mans head without the bullet possibly going through it's victim and into somebody innocent. He then turned on the other knife man who had been knocked down by the old man with the walking stick and shot him as well ,aiming up through his head again in safety for others. By this time three armed policemen on duty in the station had arrived having heard the pistol shots and were questioning the other passers by about what was going on. They then crowded around Harry pointing their pistols at him and asking him why he was armed. Harry took out his TRAPS. Identity card and showed it to the policemen who on seeing who he worked for smiled and said thank you for helping keep these people safe and saving us from a task we would have found difficult to sort out. Come back into the station with us so the people out here think you have been arrested as we know in the metropolitan police your leader Sir Cameron likes to keep his organisation a secret from the general public. Then off you can go out by a different way and we will tidy things up here. Harry said thank you and carried on managing to relax a little bit and to enjoy his walk which took him to Hyde park where he was able to see many nice statues and other things he hadn't seen before. He then made his way to an underground station and travelled to baker street where he told Sir Cameron what had happened outside the train station, whilst talking to him in his office before he then went on to receive his orders for his next task.

# Chapter Four

At the request of Sir Cameron, Harry moved to live in a second floor flat near to Finsbury Park London as this was closer to an Imam who was also   believed to be a terrorist encourager at the local mosque  that he ran and it would give Harry an opportunity to find out more about what was going on. And try to make friends with the Iman so he could pretend to be sympathetic with the Imam's beliefs and because of his possible anti British background show interest in going to a terrorist training camp in the hills between Lebennon and Syria.  Getting the support of the Imam he expected he would be accepted to it. After a few weeks of living near Finsbury park and studying the Koran as well as trying to get to know the Imam.  Harry noticed that the Imam walked past his flat on the opposite side of the road several times each day and on the days he passed after schools had closed, he was often molested by a group of teenagers not physically but with a lot of shouting and swearing and being crowded off the footpath onto the road. Again after a few weeks of witnessing this bad and frightening behaviour Harry spoke privately to the Imam and offered to intervene on his behalf which was agreed and on the next occasion it happened, Harry witnessing the gathering of teenagers, crossed the road to join the Imam.  When the row started he spoke aggressively to the young men and told them to stop what they were doing. They then turned on him and within seconds he had two of them taken by the arms and forced across to the other side of the road. He was followed by several more young men pushing and pulling as well as shouting and swearing at him and threatening to hit him. Harry aware of his capability to deal with the gang of youths pushed the two he was holding through the gate into the park and down onto the grass then he turned to the others and said, "right get on with it if you want to try and attack me". At this point one member of the gang threw a punch at him while another tried to kick him between the legs. Harry ducked to avoid the punch and at the same time caught the other's foot, pulling it upwards and back, so unbalancing the youth who he swung round to crash against the one who had tried to punch him. He then turned upon the other four who were now backing off. He ran towards them punching one lightly in the stomach and another on the shoulder then turning to the other two who now shouting the words Bloody bastard were running away, at this point he let them go and turned to the others saying, "Don't ever let me see you troubling that poor religious man again even if he has a reputation as a terrorist encourager or you will all receive more than one punch because you mustn't appear to be racist." Harry then crossed the road again to join the Imam, telling him he would in future keep an eye out for him in case he needed support again and telling the Imam he was studying the Koran would the Imam like to give him some help and advice. The answer was yes. So began a friendship between Harry and the Imam, which developed quite strongly over the weeks with Harry pretending to be very pro Islam and not only wanting to learn all about the Koran which he had already learned to recite, but also expressing the possibility of becoming an active aggressive  supporter of Islam in Britain, Harry eventually achieved what he had set out to achieve the information about terror training camps in the hills between Lebanon and Syria and other places, And asked for an invite to attend one of the ones between Lebanon and Syria so that he could learn to use the weapons of a terrorist which the Imam after a couple of days was able to give him.

Using his fake South African passport supplied by the organisation he worked for, Harry managed by traveling via Turkey to enter Syria and meet up with those the Imam had told him about who could direct him to the terrorist training camp. Harry managed to get hold of a map and a motor bike and making a note of where the camp was situated on the map so he could pass the information to Sir Cameron Later. He made his way to the camp by a motor bike he had been able to buy. Showing his papers and starting off speaking Afrikaans. He found himself welcomed to begin to join in with the lessons and because of his background appeared to learn somethings very quickly, while differently, he deliberately demonstrated badly his ability to shoot accurately so as not to allow them to think he was a former member of any military organisation. He then showed after making a few mistakes an ability to load a rifle and also how to put together explosives and fuse them to make bombs, both of which he had been shown and encouraged to learn by the instructors at the camp and became more popular with the leaders and others, because of his apparent enthusiasm for and ability to learn these activities. One of these others was a lovely looking young black woman apparently from Uganda. She too made mistakes as an apparent beginner but appeared to learn very quickly because of her enthusiasm, One day Harry had gone on his own for a fitness run and on the way back witnessed two other male members of the training group sneaking behind some of the huts in which they all lived and moving towards where the young woman was standing. Next thing he saw was one of the two men pulling out a pistol and threatening her with it, next the other man took hold of her

One of his hands around her mouth the other on her breasts and next trying to force her onto the ground with the hand on her breasts. Quickly Harry ran forward and smashed the gun from the other man's hand while at the same time the young woman had elbowed her attacker in the face and as he stepped back, raising his hands to his face, had also kicked him between the legs and was now chopping him on the back of his neck as he bent over holding himself. Harry now also chopped the other man on the neck who had been threatening the young woman with the gun. Then kicked him in the stomach as he fell to the ground. Then as the two-lay unconscious on the ground, Harry and the young woman made their way to the office cabin of the men in charge of the training camp to report what had happened, fortunately some of the other members of the trainees in the camp, who had become friends with Harry, had also witnessed what had happened although They had been too frightened of the gunman to interfere with what was happening. Now however they were prepared to speak in support of both Harry and the woman, the result was that the two men were sent from the camp told never to return to it with the threat of death if they ever misbehaved in that way again in another camp. Harry who was now ready to tell Sir Cameron exactly where the camp was which was the main part of his reason for going to it spoke to the woman suggesting that they both should leave and go back to their own countries.

The woman agreed and together they again went to the leaders and made arrangements to leave for now because of fear that some of the trainees who were friends of the other two, might secretly attack them. With the possibility of returning to another camp sometime later as they told the leaders. They both were able to set off for Lebanon, Harry on his motor bike and the woman asking to come with him on the pillion seat, so off they went, both sneaking out a pistol each and ammunition in case they should need it as they entered the wilder countryside on their way to Beirut the capitol of Lebanon.

Once in Beirut, at the suggestion of the young woman who said to Harry it would be the safest route for them to take they headed for the Israeli border. As they crossed the border the young woman went first and spoke to one of the guards on the Israeli side. After a few moments she returned together with another guard who asked Harry why he had joined the terrorists in their camp. Harry produced his passport and explained that he now lived in Britain and had managed to get an invite to the camp by making friends with an Imam and was at the camp so he could report its position to the royal air force who would be bombing it as soon as possible. The guard laughed at this and said by the time you get your message to them there won't be a camp as that is why Zala joined them and her message has been forwarded by me To our air force.

And I think we will have wiped out the camp before you even get your message home. Harry sighed and called Zala over to him and together they discussed why each had joined the camp and how they could help each other in future if necessary. After some time, they said goodbye to the guard and he allowed them to leave and continue into Israel proper.

 Once well into Israel Harry said goodbye to the young woman and arranged to meet her again in a short time. He then went to a British embassy as soon as he could so he could pass his information back to Sir Cameron as soon as possible. The camp was bombed and gunned a short time later by first the Israelis and then the RAF and the news that all had been destroyed including the terrorist trainees and the instructors was passed to Harry and his latest companion. Both harry and Zala had asked each other how come you were taking part in the Terrorist training camp, Zala answered," I am Jewish from Ethiopia and now work for Mossad" and Harry then answered, "I too work for a special service, I would like to keep our friendship strong as in future times we may again be able to help each other, or even save each other when endangered." "Yes of course said Zala, "you have already demonstrated that in my case and I care very much for you because of it." "Very good", said Harry, "I'll give you my phone number, have you got a phone number  so I could ring you".

"Yes" said Zala I'll let you have it before you leave". At this point they were passing the British Embassy, so Harry said goodbye to Zala and went in to try to make his arrangements to safely return secretly to Britain  And discuss what he had done with Sir Cameron. Zala followed him saying "I'll write my phone number down for you when I get a pen and a bit of paper" which she did and gave the paper with her number on to Harry who did the same giving his number to Zala.  A few days later having managed to get on board an aircraft he arrived in London where he attended the organisation's offices there to be again interviewed by Sir Cameron who told him to go back to his home in the Cotswolds as he didn't want the Imam to see Harry alive and so let him carry on thinking that Harry must be amongst those destroyed in the air attack on the terrorist camp. To facilitate this Sir Cameron ordered Freddie Brannigan to drive Harry home. Which he did.  About a week later the Imam whilst making one of his terrorist encouragement speeches on the steps of his Mosque was shot in the head from such a distance that no one heard the shot or could tell where it had come from. A fellow member of Harry's organisation had previously pointed out to him how about a mile away in the distance they could see a giant builders crane, apparently being used on a new estate being built.  Harry had gone to it and climbing to the top while no one was around had discovered that with his sniper's rifle spy glass he could clearly see the steps where the Iman gave his speeches and with his shooting accuracy, he could fulfil his job and remove a pro terrorist from life. Later having explained his plan to Sir Cameron and again finding an opportunity to climb the crane without being seen he carried it out. His timing was also perfect as that same day the crane was removed as the need for it in the building work was finished so no one would ever be able to notice it and think that the bullet could have been fired from it even if it seemed an impossibility because of the distance. However the death of the Iman caused a great geal of upset in the area where he gave his talks and threats were made of terrorist activity to make up for his death although no one thought that it had been an official occurrence but thought it was probably some local thug, the police also thought the same and carried out a great search of the area checking any buildings that seemed close enough and had a view of the position the Iman had been in and where people who were not Muslims lived. They were of course unable to find any evidence of a rifle shooting anywhere in the area in the properties which they had searched and announced they would also have to search Muslim inhabited properties from which the round could have been fired. In doing so they did come across a rifle which had recently been fired but were unable to prove the killer's bullet had been fired from it. However the person who lived in the flat didn't have a licence for the rifle and so he was arrested and the rifle confiscated as it was thought he could be a potential terrorist and so he ended up in prison for a short period. Which added to the strife in the area. Harry was upset by what he had caused as he believed his whole life was about preventing terrorism not encouraging it and made up his mind never to do such an open removal of a potential terrorist again but always to do such a removal in a secret way in the future. Sir Cameron agreed with this new policy of Harry's and said he would be very careful never to allow such a mistake in the future work of the terrorist raider assassination provider selection organisation or "TRAPS" as the organisation was now called for short.

# Chapter Five

one morning Harry Markham once again stood in front of Sir Cameron's large oak desk.

Sir Cameron said, "I have a very important task for you, Farid Mamoud the financial supporter of a number of terrorist organisations we want him removed permanently without it being blamed on Britain". Harry frowned then said, "but he never leaves Syria these days where he is surrounded by guards, how could I possibly take him out secretly?" "I have a plan", said Sir Cameron, "Before he became involved with terrorists, He travelled a lot and originally successfully attended Oxford university where he enjoyed playing rugby, even representing the university at one point as a winger against another University team He also had an affair with a beautiful Irish girl called Marie, this resulted in them having a daughter which they named Rima. Rima is much like her mother and very beautiful but also like her father in that she is into sport and at present attends a fencing club in Oxford. I know you were a very good fencer in your youth and also whilst in Australia you carried on with it. The coach at the fencing club she attends was a former Sergeant in the Parachute regiment called Dennis Howard, I intend to make an arrangement with him so he can find a reason not to attend the club and to replace him with you for a time long enough so you can develop a friendship with the girl. We know her father sometimes leaves Syria to stay in Paris when there is an international rugby match between France and England. If you can find out the name of the hotel where he will stay during the coming match next August, then maybe we can sort out a plan to dispose of him". Harry said yes perhaps the sergeant could pretend to have a car accident as his reason for not being able to attend the club". Sir Cameron said, "yes we will attend to it, he cycles quite a lot  and perhaps a car could appear to knock him off his bike next week some time and then you can take over, I will have a word with Dennis about this, the story will be that he will have hurt his leg" as a result of the accident. On a Monday evening at seven o'clock, ten days later Harry went to the fencing club and opened it up, when the members arrived he made an announcement of the accident that Dennis had been involved in and how for a short time he would be the coach in order to keep the club running while Dennis recovered from his injured leg which hurt a lot now but which wasn't serious enough to stop him continuing as a fencing coach after a few weeks of rest. Several members quickly got ready, put on their safety kit and began to fence each other. Harry then checked the list of those attending and called out the first name on the list for an individual lesson, a fencing speciality which most fencing coaches are pleased to carry out and which most fencers enjoy very much as part of their training.  Harry then proceeded to give the lesson commenting on the member's on guard positions in sixt and how they should keep their elbow in towards their side. After another two lessons to other members on the list, he called Rima for her lesson.  a few minutes of coaching later Harry realised, she was quite a talented fencer and told her so. Later he arranged a series of fights between different members of the club and Rima's opponent was Harry himself, throughout the fight Neither scored many hits as both were very good defensive fencers, by the end of their fight Rima had scored four hits and Harry only three, this allowed Harry to sit down with her and congratulate her on her skill, also to explain how he had managed to score his hits. Both seemed to enjoy the chat and when Harry offered a second individual lesson to take place when the others had finished and left, she was very keen to accept. The lesson went very well, Harry helped her improve her parries at first and then helped her to add a repost with each one, he also encouraged her to practice her lunge and to follow it with a quick return to the on guard position so improving her attacking ability. Rima had made a good effort in her lesson obviously enjoying herself although she now seemed very tired having worked so hard. She said to Harry, "thank you very much for this lesson it was great, Dennis gave very few individual lessons." Harry smiled and said, "you are looking very tired, how are you getting back to where you are living?" Rima replied, "Usually by bus but this late I will have to take a taxi." "Where is it you live?" asked Harry. "oh, I have a flat in Woodstock," said Rima, something Harry already knew and had been part of his plan which included getting Rima a little bit tired and a little late leaving so as he was about to leave he could offer her a lift home. "well said Harry I could offer you a lift as I have to pass through Woodstock on my way home to Kingham." Rima smiled and again said, "thank you for your kind offer I would really like to accept". "Fine," said Harry, "My car is parked at the back of the club hall. I'll just get my spare kit and weapons and we can go to it." Together they made their way out to Harry's car, Harry carrying two fencing bags while Rima carried one, at Harry's car Harry put his two fencing bags in the boot and helped Rima put hers on the back seat, so she would have to sit on the front passenger seat and Harry could chat to her. Then off they went towards Woodstock. Harry knew his way around Oxford and quickly got to the Peartree roundabout and then onto the road leading to Woodstock

After which it was a straight run to Woodstock except for a few mini roundabouts, Talking to Rima as he drove along Harry asked her where her family lived. She said "in the Middle east" "Gosh!" said Harry and did your mother or father fence?" Rima answered, "no, my mother didn't play sport she was into art and music, my father played rugby, he even played for Oxford against Cambridge." Does he still play asked Harry". "No said Rima but he loves watching it, especially internationals when England plays against France, in fact he is going to watch their match next month in Paris." "That sounds great", said Harry "will you be joining him?" Rima said, "no he will have a group of three men friends with him." Harry thought you mean armed guards but said, " that wouldn't be very good company for you, an all boys day out with lots of drinking." "There won't be any drinking of alcohol" said Rima, "we are all Moslems and keep to the rules". "Oh Gosh, "said Harry, Does he have friends in Paris to stay with?"

:no said Rima, He stays in a hotel where he and the others hire a whole floor so they can be very private, they only hire it for about a week as Paris hotels can be very expensive."

What Rima didn't know was her father did have a friend in Paris who would provide him and his guards with pistols and a special car armoured and arranged for protection.

Arriving at Woodstock Harry slowed down to thirty miles per hour to avoid breaking the speed limit as cars entered the town. "now we are here," he said, "where will I drop you off?

"would you like to join me for a coffee?" said Rima. "Thank you but not tonight said Harry but maybe on another occasion if you would still like to." Harry was being careful although he wanted a close relationship with Rima he didn't want to make it too obvious, Rima then said, "right please drop me off at the crossroads just ahead by those pedestrian lights."

Unable to stop on the main road Harry turned right into a narrow single lane street where he could stop long enough to let her out and for her to take her fencing bag with her. Before she left he asked her if she would like him to collect her for the next club meeting.

She replied, "Oh yes please there's a little street called  Union on the left just a little further on, I'll meet you there about 17 houses down just opposite the car park."  "OK. said Harry

"Shall I just drive you there now and then I'll know for sure where to meet you."  "Fine said Rima but you'll have to turn and come back this way". After letting Rima go, Harry turned the car and drove back to the central road through the town and headed for home. A week later at 5:00pm he set out for the club stopping in Woodstock to collect Rima, then heading for Oxford and the club room, he arrived at 6:45 pm and helped  Rima carry her equipment in to the club opening the door for her having first to unlock it then he went back to the car and fetched his own equipment and the equipment he loaned to the club members. A short time later the other members began to arrive and when all were signed in and began fencing with each other, Harry gave those members who asked for one their individual lessons, giving Rima her lesson towards the evening end, afterwards fencing against her for about ten minutes, he then offered her a lift home again which she accepted with delight. Driving out of oxford Harry began to talk to Rima about her dad. First he asked her how he could afford to take over a whole floor of a Paris hotel and how did he manage an education at Oxford with lessons in English. Rima smiled and said, "dad speaks very good English he learned it from his own dad who also spoke it very well, my dad also got his money from his dad who left him his business. Granddad imported Renault cars from France and sold them in Turkey. When the Turk's next began to sell Turkish cars in Europe and Arab countries, just after Turkey began to make cars.  Granddad, capable of speaking English and French as well as Turkish and Arabic. Made the Turks very Happy to use him to sell their cars. He was very successful and made a fortune from selling cars and from owning garages that serviced and repaired cars. Before he died, he gave my dad a large sum of money the equivalent of two million U.K. pounds, when he died he left his business to my dad who already spoke Arabic but had learned English French and Turkish in preparation for taking over the business which was why he came to Oxford to take a business studies degree and so continue to make the business successful which he managed to do. Since then however he has sold the business to another company in Turkey, because of the change in attitudes between Arabic countries and European ones and the problems within some Arabic countries which made him  frightened of having to travel to so many different countries to carry out his business work and also because of the development of terrorism. "Oh! GOSH!" said Harry what a shame and what a great father and grandfather you had. You're a very fortunate girl, now I know how  your father and you managed to come to Oxford to study. There are many hotels in Paris is there a particular one that your dad prefers and is that because it is good or because it is more affordable?" asked Harry. "He chooses the Novotel Suites, Paris Stade de France because it is next to the rugby ground and makes getting to the games easy." said Rima. "Oh that's very convenient "said Harry, "it sounds like the perfect place especially as it has suites, one of which your dad could book for himself and his friends."

"Yes, it is a good place, I went with him once but rugby is not a sport for me." Said Rima.

Then Harry asked, "you went with your dad once, did you enjoy the Journey even if you didn't enjoy the rugby?"  Rima smiled, "yes indeed we went first to Turkey  in a special car of dad's which he called a Peugeot 12, together with dad's friends, staying for one night in Aleppo at the Aleppo Baron Hotel, before crossing the border to Kilis and  then visiting beaches in Turkey on the way and passing through a town called Bursa, and on to Istanbul, we then travelled by plane, to Paris, where we were met by a friend of dads with a car bus called a Karson Peugeot who took us to the Novotel suites hotel, it was a smooth sunny journey and dad's friends were good fun, when we travelled from home to Istanbul, we travelled ,along the Turkish coast and visited a few lovely beaches where we stayed at some holiday huts near them, before continuing via Bursa to a ferry boat and on to Istanbul." Well, I'm pleased you enjoyed yourself even if the rugby wasn't fun", said Harry. By now they had reached Woodstock together and Harry drove slowly into the village and turned right and then left into Union Street where Rima was living. Again she invited Harry in for a cup of coffee and this time Harry accepted. Once inside the flat Rima began to make the coffee, while Harry sat in what was the lounge on a sofa. Then after about 15 minutes Rima came in carrying a tray and placed it on a coffee table by the sofa in front of Harry, then joined him on the sofa, together they sat and drank their coffee, Rima asked Harry, "where did you learn to fence?" "I started at school in South Africa", said Harry, I had wanted to do it since I was about 9 or 10 years old, when my father took me to watch a film about Zorro, called at Swords Point, I then read the book and it made me want to try fencing for myself." At this point Rima leaned against Harry and put her arm around him, Harry responded by putting his arm around her neck and allowed his hand to stroke her face, then when she turned to look at him he leaned forward and gently pulled her head towards his, then as their faces came together his mouth met hers and he gave her a long loving kiss followed by a light cuddle using both arms, he then leaned backwards pulling Rima down on top of himself and kissing her again. Rima seemed to enjoy what was happening so Harry helped her sit up and sat alongside her again, Rima then stood up and picked up the tray and cups, after taking the tray into the kitchen she returned with two more cups of coffee and a few biscuits, she placed the tray on the table again, then sat on the sofa beside Harry. Much as Harry would have liked an affair with her, he didn't want an involvement with feelings that might affect the job he had to do, so when she tried to kiss him he responded but only as far as kissing, he made no attempt to seduce her into further sexual behaviour. After a short time, Harry excused himself and left Rima, he then travelled back to his own home, enjoyed a nice drink of wine and showered and went to bed. In the morning he rang Sir Cameron and told him he had all the information that they needed about Farid Mamoud and his trip to Paris, and it was time for Dennis to return to the fencing club. Sir Cameron replied leave it with me and if you need any extra help, money weapons or manpower let me know. It is very important that we succeed, goodbye for now keep in touch, Harry now spent the rest of the day planning how he might complete the assassination, so that the guilt would not come on himself or on Britain. He couldn't just shoot at the vehicles involved as they would have been fitted with bullet proof windows and armour plating on the metal parts and on the flooring. So to use a roadside bomb would need one so powerful he couldn't be sure that in overcoming the vehicles armoured plating it wouldn't damage other cars or kill innocent people who might be nearby. Then he had a bomb plan which he was sure would work without harming any others. First, he would have to find a way to cause the car traveling to turkey to be held up for a short time on the road and to have a light weight but reasonably powerful bomb to be made with an instant radio fuse to set it off. Harry next discussed his plan with Sir Cameron to check it would work and to get the bomb made by the organisation's technicians and also tested by them to use for his plan which Sir Cameron was pleased to agree to. Next Harry had to spend time finding out how or where Mamoud's car in which he was traveling to Turkey would be or could be caused to briefly stop. Fortunately, he was able to have another chat with Rima, who said that when she had travelled to Turkey with her dad, they were held up for some time and a distance from the crossing at the border, between Syria and Turkey but some way from it by a long queue of cars. He then asked Sir Cameron to check if this was something which still happened and regularly, which Sir Cameron was able to check and confirm. So now Harry had to arrange a means of secretly getting to Syria with a bomb and A Motorbike together with another two members of Sir Cameron's team who Harry asked to be good French speakers and with false French passports just as Harry was using his false South African Passport which suited his accent and contained the  false name of Henry Mulham which he used when traveling abroad to do work for Sir Cameron, also Sir Cameron arranged Visas on their passports for countries they would enter  either on the way out or on the way back, Harry travelled across Europe to Turkey in a Ford van with a colleague called Louis, Alongside him and with the second hand motor bike in the back along with a few full petrol cans so he would later have some more petrol to make sure he had enough for the bike. Harry also carried the radio fuse for making the bomb explode. Which he carried hidden under the van to smuggle it across borders but not being attached to explosives it was easily hidden above the rear axle attached to the differential of the van. The explosive for the bomb was being smuggled into Syria by another member of the Team called Gabriel who smuggled the explosives to be used, through Saudi Arabia. Gabriel was to meet Harry at an arranged isolated spot on the out skirts of Aleppo where they would put the bomb together and place it inside a sports bag. Harry then went to Aleppo with the other team member who had travelled with him. He travelled via Killis so he could cross the border near where he intended to carry out his assassination and see what the traffic hold up was like.  It proved an ideal hold up for his plan with cars being held up for quite a long time so the queue was about a quarter of a mile long as in Harry's time lots of people from Syria liked to spend time on the Turkish beaches, so if he attacked the Mamoud car as it joined the queue he would not harm any others and still be able to go up the outside of the queue to the border without being seen to have been involved in the explosion but probably thought to be going quickly because he was frightened by it, he could make his escape across the border and keep going as far from the incident as quickly as he could. Now however he had to find where Mamoud was staying in Aleppo before continuing to Turkey, so he could follow the car to the queue at the right time on the right day. The Aleppo Baron hotel was easy to find as it was the biggest hotel there. Harry asked his colleague to go to the hotel and stay there and see if he could secretly find where the Mamoud car was parked so they would be able to follow it in the morning when Mamoud left. In the meantime, Harry contacted the team member Gabriel at the edge of the town in an isolated wild spot as arranged previously, Gabriel had the explosives which they turned into the bomb to be used and took the bomb to the van in which Harry was spending the night. In the morning Harry got ready early, he made sure the motor bike would start easily and had plenty of petrol, he also checked the bomb and the radio whose button press would make it explode. He also prepared a plastic bag of black paint which was also part of his plan and gave the van keys to Gabriel, the team member who had smuggled the explosives to him as he was to bring the van into Turkey for Harry to put the bike back into and travel back across Turkey and the rest of Europe to France and then to his home in England.  Just as he was ready the team member from the hotel came running up saying, "Mahmoud is setting out you should drive up to the road he will take and be ready for him. Gabriel who was to try to get the van into the queue just ahead of Mamoud. Left at once and Harry and his assistant colleague Louis also set out on the motor bike getting behind Mamoud's car, after a short time the van came up behind the queue followed by Mamoud's car and behind that the bike with Harry on the rear seat and Louis driving as Mahmoud's car stopped in the Queue. Harry and Louis on the bike slowly overtook it

Harry dropped the bomb bag against the side of the car just before the driver's door, not noticed by those in the car.  He then threw the bag of paint onto the windscreen which became covered by the paint, these actions being hidden from the border guards by the position of the ford van in front and stopped a little to the left side of the queue. Instantly the Mamoud car driver angrily and without thinking sprang out of the car leaving the door open and fired a pistol at the motor bike hitting Harry on his back which did no harm as the bike had speeded up and was some distance away also Harry was wearing an armoured safety vest. As he heard the pistol fire and felt the bullet hit him, he pressed the radio button and the bomb exploded and wrecked the car, killing everyone in it including the driver who had turned back to it. The bomb although small and the car armour protected, had worked because the door of the car had been left open allowing the explosion to enter it and so kill everyone. Harry's van was in front a little distance away and only slightly marked by the explosion and no vehicle close behind so no one else was hurt or other car damaged Harry and the bike driver quickly continued to the border where they were asked by the guards what they were doing and Harry explained that they had been terrified by the explosion which had happened near them and the guards believing him showed them sympathy and allowed them across without any problem and so on they went for about a mile and waited for the van to catch them up which it did after about three hours. Harry and the other two now travelled to Istanbul. Then back across Europe in the van, a very long drive during which they  slept in a number of cheap hotels or in the van on Camp sites, before arriving in Belgium and crossing the English channel and eventually arriving where they could separate and go to their homes in England by public transport, while Harry drove the van and bike to a metal recycling yard near where he lived and had them crushed and their number plates removed and cancelled. He then walked to a nearby bus stop and got a bus close to where his home was, before going to visit Sir Cameron the next morning to report the details of what had happened and where the blame would be placed. Next morning as he stood in front of Sir Cameron and began to explain the event Sir Cameron interrupted him with, "you have done a good job Harry, it looks as if the French or the Turks are going to be blamed, so you did well with that aspect of the event also the report I have received states that Mamoud and his three helpers were all killed and no one else was killed or injured, so very well done. By the way I want you to go to Northern Ireland and remove some of the Terrorist leaders and bomb makers on both sides. Could you do that? I'm sure you can as you make very good plans for dealing with difficult situations and being South African on your false passport will enable you to become friendly with people from both sides and get to know who the leaders are and other specialists. What do you think?" I think it will suit me as I like removing Terrorists of all kinds because of what terrorists did to my family. So OK. But I will need a lot of help from you, especially as I will want to fly there in my own plane so I can flee back to England should I need to." "Fine," said Sir Cameron, "I will do all that you ask of me to help you also should you need any more team members to help I'll also send them to aid you." "Thank you," said Harry, "let's go ahead and make the arrangements".

# Chapter Six

Settled nicely at home one evening Harry Markham was enjoying a nice glass of wine and watching a program on television about football, when his work phone rang, he went to his office to answer it, thinking it must be about his work and another task from Sir Cameron. However to his surprise it was a female voice with a foreign accent when the person said hello to him and it turned out to be Zala the member of the Mossad he had met while at the terrorist training camp in the hills between Lebanon and Syria where he had managed to go to find it's exact position so that the RAF could bomb it and prevent the development of more terrorists and where he had saved Zala from attempted rape by two of the other male trainees. After which he became a good friend of hers, discovering she his was there for a similar reason to his, except her reason was to provide Mossad with the information to enable them to destroy the camp. After they had both left the camp and discussed with each other why they were there. He had exchanged phone numbers with her in case they would ever again need to meet, in order to help each other. After their hellos to each other Zala said to him, "I am ringing to ask you for some help Harry, There is a former Irish bomb maker who is now living in England and he has been offered a large sum of money to come and teach some of our terrorist neighbours here in Israel, how to make bombs to fit in suit cases and hand bags and we know he has accepted the award and will soon be coming to fulfil the job. I have been sent to try and take him prisoner and place him on a Jewish ship that will be mooring near Dartmouth, so we can remove him before he can join our enemies. Helping them to cause us problems in our towns just like those carried out by the IRA In the early seventies in Belfast. Would you be able to help or even advise me as what to do." Harry answered with, "yes indeed do you want me to remove him for you? If so do you know where he is living at present?"

Zala replied, "he is currently living in a house in a row of new houses in a town called Chipping Norton and I have to have him taken by my people in the boat so we can take care of him and we can question him in order to find out where the people employing him are operating from". "His home is very convenient ," said Harry, it is near to where I am  living at present and I will try to buy a house in the same street, then I 'll tell you the remainder of the plan I have in my mind, for taking him secretly as a prisoner to Dartmouth harbour, when I meet you at the house." Harry after saying "goodbye and I'll be in touch again in a few days," rang off and then rang

Sir Cameron to tell him what was going on and to ask him if he could supply

the money to buy the house for his plan. Sir Cameron said," yes he would provide the cash to buy the house as it would be good to get rid of a bomb maker but the house once bought would belong to the organisation not Harry and would be resold when Harry had carried out his plan." Harry agreed and said it would be available in a few months for resale when he had finished helping remove the bomb maker and now the cash would be needed in about a week to finish buying it. In three weeks, Harry wascontacted by Zala again, who was already in England and Harry asked her to meet him in the Coop store in Chipping Norton in three days' time, and then together they would go to live in the house he had bought pretending to be a pair of lovers. Zala hesitated for a few seconds then agreed provided Harry promised not to attempt to take advantage of her in the house without her agreement.  Harry said he would be pleased to do as she asked and he would behave himself while they lived together. So Zala agreed to meet him in three days' time in the Coop store. After meeting they both went to the House that Harry had bought. The house had a nice front garden with a high hedge along part of the front of it. Harry and Zala went inside together and sat down on the sofa that Harry had moved into it along with several matching armchairs and lots of other necessary furniture as well as bedroom furniture and kitchen equipment. Harry asked her would she like a cup of coffee or a glass of wine. Zala said, "I would like to have the coffee please," Harry then went into the kitchen and prepared the coffee, two cups of which he brought out on a tray together with a plate of fruit cake and set them on a coffee table in front of the sofa and then sat down himself. They sat together on the sofa and discussed Harry's plan to Kidnap the Irish neighbour from 5 houses away. First they had to invite him into their house then drug him and sneak him out to their car and then take him to Dartmouth to where the Jewish ship was moored. How could they get a stranger to enter their house was the question Zala asked Harry. Harry replied, "you should start doing some work in the front garden and see if your beauty can interest him when he walks past, then when he speaks to you, you can show him friendship and one day a bit later on you can invite him in for a cup of coffee". Next day during late morning Zala started to work on the front garden at about the time they had noticed their bomb maker neighbour walked past, almost each day probably to go shopping and as he passed she looked up and smiled at him receiving a "good morning Miss from him" in a strong northern Irish accent, to which she replied, "thank you neighbour and good morning to you." She then carried on working in the garden with the result that after a few days the Neighbour was saying good morning even when Zala was still gardening and not looking up.

A few more days during which some short friendly conversations about Ireland and it's problems had taken place as well as about Uganda which Zala knew about and they had exchanged names.

One day Zala was up a ladder wearing a pair of tight shorts and a top which showed off her lovely breasts.

When the neighbour in passing said good morning Zala to her, She came down the ladder a large welcoming smile on her face and asked him "Sean would you like to join me for a cup of tea or coffee?" to which he replied, "yes thank you very much." "I was thinking of inviting you for a drink in my house." Together they entered the house and sat on the sofa to be greeted by Harry who asked, "what would each of you like to drink?" Zala explained to Sean that Harry was her very free thinking lover from Africa, so Sean was very welcome in the house. Sean relaxed and asked Harry for a cup of strong tea which Harry went into the kitchen to prepare and returned after ten minutes with a cup of coffee for Zala and one for himself as well as the cup of tea and some biscuits for Sean, he also brought a plate of fruit cake for them all to eat with their drinks, Harry began to tell Sean about how he felt over the British attitude to Rhodesia and Sean spoke about the division of Ireland and how it came about just after the government in Dublin managed to become independent from Britain because at that point many protestants had had their homes burnt by the IRA, having been accused of being traitors. Causing them to flee to the North of the country out of fear. There joining together with the larger number of protestants who lived in that area. Then because of their loss of homes and fear of the IRA the fleeing Southern families encouraged the northern protestants to demand a complete division from the Dublin government which they were eventually able to achieve and so a border was created dividing Ireland into two parts a smaller mainly protestant northern part and a larger mainly catholic southern part. Shortly after finishing his drink the drug which Harry had put in it began to work and Sean quickly became unconscious. Harry and Zala quickly tied his hands and feet together and Harry slipped another drug tablet into his mouth to help keep him unconscious. Then as soon as it was dark and the street quiet, they wrapped him in a rug carried him out and put him in the boot of their car, before driving to Dartmouth which meant a reasonably long drive across country, then down the M5 motorway which they left before driving to Totnes, before carrying on and arriving at Dartmouth. On arrival Zala radioed the Jewish ship for a small boat to come to the shore after dark and from there be able to take their prisoner on board. This arrived at the dock side after some time and just as it had become dark,  with darkness and no people around. The still unconscious prisoner was put on board the small rowing boat and sent on his way to the waiting Israeli ship. On board which he  was to travel as a prisoner all the way to Israel where he would be questioned about the people who had tried to employ him, to pass his bomb making knowledge onto them, Harry and Zala then headed back home again this time to Harry's own house in Kingham, where they each went to bed, each in their own bedroom. Next morning Harry rang Sir Cameron and told him the Plan was complete and the house in Chipping Norton could be sold any time he wanted to sell it.  Sir Cameron replied with, "thank you for letting me know, now it is time for you to start doing the main part of your job, that is getting rid of all known terrorists we cannot gain enough evidence against to Jail for life. Pop in and see me to discuss the plans in the morning as early as you can. This gave Harry a jolt, how could he kill a number of known but not prosecuted terrorists without it causing a major racist problem and perhaps even encourage more terrorists, then he thought of Zala and the ship moored off the coast if he could get a ship like that then he could place the bodies on it and have them trans ported out to the Atlantic and dumped,as a better method than the one he used which meant he had to fly a plane across to the Atlantic every time he killed one or two evil persons  how was he to do this?  If he was having to kill a large number of evil people at the same time. He began to try and think it through.

 He thought of buying a fishing boat but he would have problems getting a crew who wouldn't object to doing it and who he could trust not to let the secret out. Then he thought of his ability to fly and if he could have use of a larger private airfield of his own instead of paying rent for a small one and Flying a not very big private aircraft but one still big enough to hold a couple of bodies or four. The plane that he currently used being a Dakota which was able to fulfil what he needed  and  was not too difficult to take off and land on the private airfield he used at present. Using his Dakota he could fly the dead bodies together with a colleague helper who had the job of oprning a door and pushing the dead bodies out over the Atlantic and drop them in well away from the land, so the bodies would be eaten by fish before they could arrive on the shore. Living as he did in the Cotswolds Harry wondered if he could get access to a  a suitable boat moored on the South coast of England somewhere suitable for his needs if Sir cameron when he sold the house in Chipping Norton could be persuaded to buy one.

If Sir Cameron when he sold the house in Chipping Norton could be persuaded to buy a  boat for him suitable for the job and also employ some new colleagues capable of  motoring out around Ireland and well into the Atlantic.  When asked and had it explained, Sir Cameron hesitatingly agreed to look into the suitability and the possibility of arranging it. He did mention that Harry already had obtained a small motor driven yacht from the smugglers he had killed and asked Harry to search out the right place which was going to be suitable

To moor it and where no one would notice the bodies being placed on to it. Harry got on with looking into all the requirements and decided that the current method whould cause him much less trouble as it was operated by himself and was close to where he lived as well as being easy to place the bodies into without anyone else seeing what was happening. Harry also thought maybe he could place more bodies in to the plane if he had a good look at the space and check if he could place them on top of each other. Sir Cameron After a little time said, there is already a private airfield near where you live which you are using. Why should you want something different when you have no problems with the current method you are using as you have persuaded the owners to let you use the airfield for yourself whenever you want to and offered them a rent if they would agree, which they were happy to agree to. It is only important that we mustn't let them know what your job is and what you will be carrying on the plane. Should you need a bigger plane capable of carrying more bodies then you would be better keeping some bodies for a short time in the house you live in or a shed in your garden and then make more flights taking just as many bodies each time as fit in to your present plane. Harry answered with, " it does work good and having thought more about it. I don't need anywhere else

The one I use now Requires little effort from me, I"LL let you know each time I use it and how much rent I must pay for each flight to it and from it. I have sorted out a special pass with those in charge so that when I go in with a body in my car no one will want to search my car or ask me what I am doing. After speaking to those in charge of the private airfield and getting them to agree to let me have use of it for more than a few occasional flights to other parts of Britain I might not need a bigger plane however if we increase the size of the plane and start arriving in a van instead of a car they may ask what has changed with what I have been doing. I will have to have a good excuse to give them. Now having informed his leader Sir

Cameron, the head of the committee for the study of the causes of terrorism and the causes of terrorist behaviour, who now explained to Harry that he would let him have some extra income to pay for any extra rent of the private airfield. Harry to keep secret, his true reason for having his own plane had explained to the private air field owners when asked why he was using his own plane, that he owned an aeroplane as part of his back ground  from Rhodesia now called Zimbabwe and wanted somewhere near where he lived to keep it and fly it as he didn't want to lose his flying ability and licence and also because he had a friend who lived near Newtownards in Northern Ireland where there was another private airfield he could use as it had already been arranged by his friend so it would be a reasonable way to go and visit him now and again. Harry hadn't told the owner that he also had a special arrangement with a Sir Cameron who would arrange his flight plans for him but didn't mention to the owner what the plans were, because they were when he needed to fly safely out over England to the coast, then North up the Irish sea and round the Northern Irish coast to the Atlantic. If asked why he was going that way.  He was ready to say that he was hoping to have a view over the Atlantic and the Irish coast there before traveling back to Newtonards to visit his friend. The real reason being as part of his job, so he could fly out far enough to drop off bodies without there being any chance of them being washed ashore. And then making a safe return journey to the private airfield. The airfield owners were reasonably understanding of Harry's reasons for wanting to use their private airfield and accepted his use of it with what seemed a certain amount of pleasure.

# Chapter Seven

Following instructions from Sir Cameron. Harry had to find a way to travel to and remain in Belfast Northern Ireland and start to remove terrorists. Of which there were many, on the sides of both the catholic and protestant peoples. Something Harry proceeded to do with enthusiasm as he had suffered a huge upset following the action of terrorists killing all the other members of his immediate family when he lived in southern Rhodesia as Zimbabwe was called   until 1980. Harry looking forward to removing lots of terrorists started to follow Sir Cameron's orders, by planning to  use his knowledge and ability gained as a member of the Selous Scouts, To kill the terrorist leaders in Belfast and use his licence to fly aeroplanes which he had gained while living in Australia  to travel to Northern Ireland in his Dakota plane provided by Sir Cameron for use as part of Harry's usual job as an assassin of terrorists.  The plane was normally used by Harry to dispose of the bodies of terrorists killed secretly in England. This was done by Harry flying the bodies a fair distance out over the Atlantic and dropping them into the sea. The plane which Harry normally kept on a private airfield near where he lived he now intended using for safety reasons to travel to an airfield near Newtownards where he intended leaving it parked ready to use should he need to flee back home for any reason. And using his motor bike which he was able to fit into the plane, to travel to Belfast on and therefore be able to use the bike as a secure means with which to return to the airfield in a hurry should he need to.

Harry now known as Henry Mulham on his fake South African passport. A name he chose as it meant he couldn't mix his Initials when spoken to under pressure and the Name was similar to his real name so for himself easily remembered and pronounced, and his signature remained very similar to what it had been. He was also acting as a South African because he could control that accent and speak Afrikaans with little trouble or thought as well as knowing much about the history of South Africa.  These things would help to keep him safe in Northern Ireland wherever he went, should it be a protestant area or a catholic area as it would be thought that he was neither. His first home was a rented flat, in a street just off the Newtownards Road in Belfast, which thanks to one of his colleagues who came from Northern Ireland ,telling him what to do he was able to arrange easily and quickly on his arrival. Living there he was able to get to know some of the protestant thugs of the UDA and prepare how to deal with them. He got to know them by first playing side drum in one of the local flute bands which  meant he became friendly with lots of local people as the band was well known and took part in  the twelfth of July  marches. Side drum playing being one of the things he had enjoyed doing at the college he attended in South Africa. Harry being a little unusual in the district was invited to several meetings with the UDA members in a local public house to have a drink and to discuss his African background as well as also discuss Northern Ireland and it's history with them. Harry was able to tell them about the Boer rebellion against Britain. He discovered that they behaved as they did because like Harry they had lost innocent members of their families  killed by terrorists, except in their case it was caused by  bomb attacks carried out in Belfast city,  in large busy shops and also in the  major market or on buses. Harry told them that he was originally from Rhodesia and how he had lost his mother, father and brother in a terrorist attack and had gone to live in South Africa as a result of this,  so he personally could  be safer, which earned him the sympathy of the UDA members and also made Harry sympathetic towards them  which brought a closer relationship and made Harry feel so sorry for them that rather than do them any harm he thought perhaps he should be helping them. During his conversations with them he told them how he had learned to play the side drum in a college in South Africa as a young boy. All This free chatting gave Harry a chance to talk about the U.D.A. and who the main and leading members were, he also learned from them that one of the early leading rebels against England had been a protestant called Wolf Tone  and that the division of Ireland had been brought about by the behaviour of the IRA in the 1920s.when the IRA frequently set up ambushes in the southern counties of Ireland against the English army the police and the Black and Tans,  when an ambush went wrong  because those being ambushed seemed to know what was about to happen, they blamed the local protestants whom they considered traitors and drove them from their homes then set fire to their houses. The protestant families now very badly frightened and with nowhere to live. Fled to the north of the country where they knew more protestants lived and persuaded the protestants they met there that they should remain part of the union with the UK and separate the north area of Ireland from the South for their safety's sake which the protestants eventually managed to do successfully thanks to the help of Baron Carson.  Once Harry found out the names of the UDA leaders he soon found out where the homes of the leaders where and where they got together to plan their attacks.  Hearing these tales and having sympathy for the members of the UDA who had lost innocents from their families as Harry had, Harry decided to leave the area and changed his mind about removing any members of the UDA from life. He then left the area for a neutral one not so far away, which was part of the nearby Castlereagh Road, towards the outer end of it before the business area of factories and a little way from the council estate where George Best grew up, He was lucky in that he found another nice place to live in a flat above a shop which he rented.  After about six months to allow time to clear his past contact with the Ulster defence Association, his next place to move to was to be in a Catholic area called The Ardoyne, where the Catholic terrorist organisation known as

Irish Republican Army had members. This time after he moved and found a comfortable place to live, in a rented flat in the area where he wanted to get to know people. He found himself a job working as a collector and deliverer for a local laundry company. Living in a flat amongst the local people he soon made friends with and got to know many ordinary people. Apparently coming from South Africa, he let those he talked to believe he was from a background neutral as regards protestant or Catholic but potentially anti British because of what had happened to South Africa's neighbour Rhodesia although this time he didn't disclose that he was originally from Rhodesia himself, this enabled him to meet a few of those who were IRA terrorists, After moving from the Protestant area Harry informed Sir Cameron of the U.D.A. he had found out about and told Sir Cameron how they had been upset by terrorism just as Harry himself had been and that Harry couldn't bring himself to do them any harm as he had every sympathy for them. Sir Cameron more concerned that the UDA where also killing innocents and not making the situation in Northern Ireland better, decided to send other members of the "TRAPS "association to sort them and told Harry to concentrate on the IRA. Harry had also asked Sir Cameron to supply him with a special ion scanner before he flew to Newtownards. A scanner which when placed near something that had touched explosive material or which had been close to explosive material and had picked up the smell of it, the ion scammer would indicate that fact. Once he was ready to use the gadget Harry could check all the laundry he collected and know the name and address of those who had handled explosives or fired a gun of some sort and enable him through his friendships and gossip with local people to further check them as he didn't want to assassinate someone who had just been clay pigeon shooting or perhaps worked as a game keeper or some other way had an innocent contact with a gun or explosive material. Once certain that someone was a terrorist Harry then placed on the clothes he had to return to them from the laundry the poison which he had brought with himself, having had it made by the scientists who worked for his organisation. he had first used this poison on the clothes of terrorists while fighting them in Rhodesia as a member of the Selous Scouts.  He then delivered the poisoned clothing which he knew had had a contact with explosive material when he returned the laundry, After a few weeks of delivering the poisoned clothes he began to realise he might be beginning to be suspected as the cause of the deaths that would suddenly be occurring and also began to carry his pistol as he went about, expecting the possibility of an attack. To his horror on one occasion as he was returning some laundered clothes which he had discovered  had been in contact with explosives he noticed a couple of men entering  the house he was parked close to as he  had just delivered poisoned clothes to it and wondered what they were doing, next they came rushing back out of the house  before Harry could drive off as he had been also returning some laundered clothes to a neighbouring house. Seeing the two men walking quickly along the footpath towards his van, he quickly got out of his van, first picking up his pistol and preparing for an attack. He then noticed the two men  turn towards his van and he also noticed one producing a pistol from inside his jacket, with that Harry leaving the van door open nipped around the back of the van and forward along the other side to stand protected by the engine on the passenger side,  taking out his own pistol and holding it out of sight against the side of the van as the two men came closer, he was ready if necessary to raise his pistol and fire it, He wondered if they were terrorist friends of the terrorist he had just returned the laundry to or if they could be police inquiring about the sudden death of a number of people living in this street, Consequently he called out to them, "what do you want?" Hoping if they were police they would say so and produce their badges or ask him to put his hands up and come out from behind the car, the two men answered him by the unarmed one taking out a pistol and the armed one firing his pistol at  Harry who was saved by the van engine taking the shot then Harry raising his pistol shot the one with the pistol in his hand, the other man having pulled out his pistol began firing it at Harry who fortunately was again  protected a little by the van engine behind the bonnet. Harry then running with bent legs to keep himself hidden by the van ran around the back of it and shot the other man on the side of his head. He then quickly boarded the van and drove away at a speed not so fast as to attract attention and headed off towards his aeroplane, arriving safely about a mile from  the air field, he abandoned the van in a side of the road car rest and using his motorcycle which he carried in the van just in case he needed to secretly approach his aeroplane, he made his way to the airfield, He then fled the country in his private plane  from the small airfield near Newtownards to his secret home in Britain, knowing he had removed a good number of terrorists and he would probably be hunted by both the police and any remaining Terrorists. Some weeks later Harry was again interviewed by Sir Cameron, who explained to him that his colleagues,  none of whom were from Northern Ireland, had removed a few leading Protestant terrorists and the IRA had been blamed for it. Also 12 known IRA bomb makers or leaders had been poisoned somehow along with some members of their families who could have been innocents, as well as two armed terrorists shot and killed, all of which a foreign man was being blamed for, these are the results of your work and information. Harry frowned and said you are right they are the results of my work which in the case of the UDA has made me unhappy and in the case of the innocent members of the IRA has also upset me and is making me wonder if what I am doing as a job is really any different than being a terrorist myself. Anyway I won't be able to return to Ireland again as they will be searching for me and I could either be shot by terrorists or end up arrested and sent to prison by the local police it was always my plan to make sure Briton wasn't to be blamed for removing the terrorists as that would have encouraged more terrorism over here in Britain from those remaining or even caused more people to have sympathies for them and join them and so make things worse instead of better. What he hadn't considered was that all foreign single male visitors to Northern Ireland would now be treated with suspicion. Instead of welcomed.

# Chapter Eight

Although taking part in a job which involved the killing of terrorists and those who supported them by financing and encouraging them as well as treating those of other evil behaviour in the same way. Harry in spite of this was keen to be friendly and helpful to his neighbours and those he met in his free time activities which mainly were his long walks on the Malvern's which he liked to do early during evenings when he was able to return from the TRAPS offices in London early or in the afternoons when he didn't have to go to the offices  and was able to visit a local pub for a drink with a few locals with whom he chatted about his past in Rhodesia telling them about all the good things available for him, including his education at a college in South Africa his activities at home his good if somewhat far away neighbours and the pleasure he had before the attack on his parents and then about what had happened. When asked about his present job he described it using the original title of the organisation and so made friends. He was also very successful at making friends because of his willingness to help them if asked and chat and invite them to enjoy a drink with him as well as join him on his walks. He was also very friendly and supportive of his colleagues who he worked with and they in turn were always ready to be helpful to him as well as to each other. Harry was particularly popular because of his technical abilities and his planning abilities which helped the organisation to find removal solutions of terrorists their supporters and other evil people, in as secret a way as possible so as to keep public blame away from the organisation.

Living in his large house near to Kingham in the Cotswolds Harry had made close friends with those who lived near him, one of whom was Richard Welldean the manager of a bank in the nearby town of Chipping Norton, who Harry visited from time to time at Richard's office in the bank as well as at his family home, where Richard had a very friendly wife with a new young daughter and two older sons. On one occasion that Richard had taken his three-year-old daughter with him to work and had her upstairs in his office with him. She was playing with some toys sitting on the floor while her dad did some paperwork. Suddenly at about 12:30pm. a young man and a young girl entered the bank having pulled up on a motorbike outside and each still wearing their helmet and mask The young man produced a pistol and pointing it at a cashier handed over a note demanding twenty thousand pounds. The cashier safely protected by her bullet proof glass and counter merely tore up the paper and got ready to press a button which set off an alarm which the police would hear and as the  Police station was only about  a quarter of a mile away they would arrive in just a few minutes in their car. Then the young man trying to frighten the cashier fired the pistol at the ceiling and pointed it at one of the bank customers. Then dashing outside with his female partner when the cashier pressed the alarm button. The two crooks together leaped onto their motor bike and drove off as quickly as they could. Then the bank manager arrived downstairs tears in his eyes," are you OK sir," said the cashier. "yes", said the manager," but some fools bullet struck my baby daughter and killed her". At that moment Harry Markham entered the bank to speak to his friend.

 " Oh! No!" said Harry as he overheard the conversation, "I'll help you Richard, to find the culprit's

And deal with things as best I can to help bring you support and relief." "great and many thanks," said the cashier to Harry, on the  bank manager's behalf "I'll give you all the information that I can to help you make a start, They came by motorbike a young man and a young woman, he armed with a pistol and trying to rob the bank. Then when he realised that I as the cashier wasn't frightened of him and not going to obey him, probably because he realised that I was protected by bullet proof glass above the counter as well as steel behind the lower boards of my counter, he tried to frighten me by firing the pistol in the air, he then fled when he saw me press the button on my counter.

And heard the alarm sounding outside the bank. Knowing the police would soon be here as their station wasn't far away.

It is believed that the two crooks went off in the direction of Banbury and the police having arrived here and discovered what had happened immediately went after them hoping to catch up with them or find out where they lived. By going to Banbury they had to pass the police car which is why the police were not able to get after them so quickly as they were already coming this way after the button press and then after coming in to find out what was happening had to turn their car in the busy town traffic. It being the only car the local police have. Our police having only a car not motor bikes they will probably find it impossible to catch the two crooks, given the narrow backroads and cross country tracks the two crooks could have taken, but by our police by getting in touch with Banbury police which was the direction the two crooks went in initially they may well be able to discover where the two thugs live and get the Banbury police to set up a traffic halts on the most likely entry points to the town that the crooks would use."I knowing also that it was not unlikely they would need to watch on the less used entrances to the town should the crooks turn off the main road to the town and take one of the country roads on it's left hand side and sneak into Banbury by another entrance. Probably one near where they lived and so be able to manage to return home and hide. What wasn't known by anyone unfortunately was that the Pair had left a car parked in a layby on the main Chipping Norton to Banbury road and had been far enough ahead of the police at that point to enable them to pull over and leave the bike behind the hedge in the field next to it and take off in the car and drive slowly home without  worry or drawing any attention to themselves as the police overtook them hoping to catch the two on the motorbike, not knowing they had swapped it for a car and hidden it behind the hedge.

 Harry however Had just returned from Banbury, a short time before he entered the bank to speak to his friend. he had gone to shop in Banbury at one of the superstores there so that he could get the food he really liked to eat. On the way to Banbury he had noticed a white car parked in a lay by and much later again on the way back he had noticed the same white car still parked in the layby which was situated a long way from any houses or a place that someone would want to visit.  There was also no cross country walk paths in that area and at the time Harry wondered why anyone would have left a car parked there so long, when seeing it for the second time he thought it might have broken down so took the number in case  later he would want to help someone with a what he thought was a broken down car and would need to be able to trace the owner.

 His suspicious mind made him wonder if it had anything to do with the two crooks so he decided to have a look at the layby as part of his enquiries and also as he was going to go to Banbury to see what he could find out for himself. Approaching the layby, he noticed the car had gone and so stopped to have a look around. Again being Harry and used to working in the bush he decided to look beyond the layby into the field and soon found a motor bike in the field some distance from the road next to another hedge where it was hidden under a pile of cut down hedge branches and old hay. There was a number plate on it so he took the number and left it at that and drove off heading for Bretch Hill Banbury a place which he had heard about from some of his friends as an area where young people were thought to be quite naughty, he thought it possible a wicked couple might have found somewhere to live there which is what he thought the two crooks might be.

Driving slowly through the streets of the estate he eventually saw the same white car as the one he had seen parked in the layby. He stopped near it, first checking his silenced pistol was loaded and got out of his car. He had found the white car he was searching for parked outside a block of flats. He went into the hall of the block and knocked on the first flat door he came to, after a short wait this door was opened by an elderly woman who he asked did she know who owned the car outside and did she know of a young couple who lived in the flats. Her answer was most helpful, "yes she did know who owned the car, her grandson who was part of a young couple who lived in flat 14 on the first floor". Harry said thank you and walked out of the block and sat in his car for a while. Before returning and going upstairs to number 14 and knocking on the door, he had looked at the names and flat numbers on the board outside. And found that flat 14 was inhabited by a Charles Simpson and flat 8 on the ground floor was where a Lilian Simpson lived and was the flat he had spoken to the grandmother in. He knocked on the door of number 14 and it was opened by a young man. Harry reached out and took the young man by the neck putting pressure on his pressure points, until the young man passed out, then carrying him he entered the flat and seeing a sofa laid him down on it. Following his semi violent entrance Harry checked the flat for others, coming across a young girl sitting in the kitchen. "right," Harry said, "your boyfriend is lying next door on the sofa

If you want to see him alive again you had better answer my questions, are you the two people who raided the bank in Chipping Norton?" the girl turned her head and faced Harry,

"yes she said but we had to flee as the pistol went off accidently"
Harry smiled and said "thank you, good bye, where is the pistol?'
we threw it away somewhere on the drive back" she said.

Harry left the flat at this point, he then returned home as quickly
as he could and telephoned his friend the bank manager asking
him to tell the local police where the two crooks involved in the
Chipping Norton bank raid lived and that they should look in the
two post boxes in the flat block which had the name of Simpson
on them in case the pistol might be hidden in one of them.
thinking that similar post boxes were a place that he would hide
his pistol if he didn't want anyone to find it. Harry also thought
that the pistol might be hidden rather than thrown away and lost
forever. he said that they should do this as soon as possible, The
manager said he would tell the police straight away and
encourage them to do the search, without mentioning how he
knew. The local police raided the flat and found the pistol in the
Lilian Simpson post box, and  testing the marks on the bullet
fired in the bank and the inside of the pistol barrel, proved it was
the one used in the raid .having checked that it was the one from
which the bullet was fired that killed the little girl. After a little
further careful checking, Matching fingerprints of the two crooks
were found on the pistol however they would have to ask
witnesses to help prove for sure the young man and woman in
flat 14 were the two involved in the killing so would have to
speak to all those who were in the bank at the time and have a
line up and eye witness inspection. Thanks to Harry's help and
the eye witness help of the bank customers which was doubtful
due to the two thugs wearing their motor cycle helmets and
goggles but some  of the witnesses including those  who had
received a description from Harry. Harry who unknown to the
police had spoken to the girl and seen the young man in the flat
and so could recognise them as a result had described them to
some of the other witnesses who did chose the two involved and

the police soon had the two in court where they were found guilty of felony murder and sent to prison for life with a minimum sentence of twenty five years for each of them.

Harry then went to visit his bank manager friend Richard who together with his wife, was still suffering at the death of his daughter. Harry assured them that he would visit the two young thugs if they came out of prison after twenty five years or especially if they came out before the twenty five years were up as often happened and punish them properly and make sure they could never do anything like this again, with removal from life permanently. The couple who were crying and still very upset by the death of their baby daughter. Said to Harry while we understand what you are planning we realise that this is something that would bring the terrible unhappiness that we are suffering to their parents and are now satisfied with what you have done and that they will be spending a long time in prison. which hopefully will correct their future behaviour and not put you in the risk of also ending up in prison. And possibly destroying your life.

# Chapter Nine

Following an order from Sir Cameron, Harry Markham had a non-terrorist job to do, this time it was to deal with foreign drug smugglers from South America and Harry who had a very good ability to learn foreign languages had already learned while still at school to speak quite a good form of Spanish.  Which was why he had been asked to find out who the drug suppliers  were and if necessary, go to their home countries and assassinate them. In the Meantime  word had been obtained  about a meeting with the British drug traffickers and their foreign suppliers by other members of the organisation who had pretended to be drug traffickers and got to know and become friends with real traffickers, the meeting was to be  between the group of British Drug traffickers and their  suppliers, in an old barn which had been tidied up for use as a business centre near a small Essex village which was renowned for it's beauty and where strangers would not attract attention as there were always lots of visitors coming to the village just to see it and the village people were very friendly and didn't interfere with or bother visitors. Aso the nearest police station was quite a long way away and the village which depended on visitors for it's income had only a local man as it's own policeman, who he tended to support the village whenever he could. This meant, that In order to support the village he didn't bother visitors unless he knew they had actually done something wrong in the village. Harry with one of his colleagues was watching what was happening with orders to remove as many of the smugglers as he could. He saw  six of the British traffickers arrive in a smart black Jaguar car and watched them park by the barn and go into it. Harry together with his colleagues who had already pretended to be Traffickers, went into the barn which had been filled with comfortable seats and a raised platform at one end. There they watched and listened to the foreign suppliers addressing their audience of British traffickers.  They also Took note of the countries and cities or towns the suppliers came from as well as doing as much as they could to obtain the names of the British dealers and secretly photographing them with hidden cameras so that they might remove them at a later date.  Having seen the direction the Jaguar had come into the village they were using. Harry and one of his friends left the meeting just before it seemed to be ending and went to their own car. There Harry armed himself with his sniper's rifle and went into a field outside the village, alongside the road he expected the Jaguar to drive out along. As it was the road it came to the village in

He made sure he had a spot with good view of the road which was very narrow and had difficult bends to pass around and there he settled down with the rifle which he aimed at a part of the road along which a car driver would not want to travel very fast.

Then when he saw the Jaguar coming back along the road, he got ready to fire a shot at it and send a tracer round into the petrol tank. Something he managed to do, causing the tank to explode wrecking the car and killing everyone in it. Then together with his friend they went and joined their colleagues, then fled across the field and back to their own car and quickly driving off to report their actions to Sir Cameron.  Sir Cameron was much annoyed at the report telling Harry, it was the suppliers In this particular case I wanted you to mainly get rid of, now you will have to follow them back to their own countries and deal with them there, more problems and greater expense. Yes, said Harry but we won't have to deal with more problems here including potential terrorism from their friends and supporting cartels. Best if I deal with them in their own countries if possible. "OK." Said Sir Cameron," where will you go to first and what will you need?"  "I will have to go to Colombia as that is where the main speaker and provider came from, I know which city he works from and will go there and remove him and as many of his cartel members as I can without being known to have done it.  I will need to smuggle in a radio rocket  attracter and have a small rocket to be launched from an aircraft into his office when he is having a cartel meeting, I will need the rocket attractor to help fired rocket it to be accurate, I will need to be at the meeting to make sure what is happening and how long it will continue for, so I can set up the removal of the cartel members as well as the head man, then get some little distance from the meeting myself so as to stay safe. "Fine", said Sir Cameron, "you will have to sneak carefully into the country if you are going to take in a rocket attractor in case the customs search you", Two months later Harry had got himself into Colombia by getting a journey on a destroyer going to help at Belize, his joining it was arranged by Sir Cameron and then Harry was able to leave it while it was still some distance out at sea and he sneaked into Columbia by rowing a small dinghy to the shore of Columbia and once on shore pulling it into the nearby jungle and hiding it there.  He had made sure there was no evidence of it having been a British boat before bringing it on board the destroyer, Having arrived safely on shore and hidden the boat Harry could now Keep the  radio rocket attractor hidden safely in his bag of spare clothes and sneak through the bush to Medellin where he intended to live in a hotel near to where he expected the head drug exporter to hold his cartel meeting. A few hours later Harry had used the information he had previously gained at his meeting with the chief drug exporter in the small English village. To enable him to work out where this man who was the drug cartel leader was going to hold his meeting and had made his way to a hotel that was near to it and also as it happened near the outskirts of the town and booked a room in it for a week. Next day he made his way to a third-floor office in a tall building across the road from the hotel and a little way along it further towards the outskirts of Medellin and went into the office to join the meeting. The leader of the cartel recognised him from the meeting in Essex and Harry said he had come to prepare a large order of drugs, during the next few days, to be smuggled into Britain. Consequently he was welcomed with a wave and a smile. Harry stood at the rear of the meeting by the window and with everybody concentrating on the leader managed to place the rocket attractor, contained in a small plastic bag he had carried with his left hand, behind the window curtain on the ledge, it was further hidden by being placed behind a number of flower pots also on the window ledge. After about 20 minutes Harry gave a wave to the leader and saying, "I'll contact you again soon." left the meeting, this was understood as the meeting was now in Spanish and Harry was thought not to understand what was being said. Harry quickly returned to his hotel room and then taking his radio with him went out to the nearest piece of jungle and radioed the Ark Royal on which was an American made F4 Phantom.  A plane which had been previously sold to Britain by the United States of

America. Consequently this plane had no country markings on it, instead it had it's tail painted blue so other British planes would recognise it if necessary. Harry was doing this because Sir Cameron had arranged with the RAF to carry out Harry's plan of firing a plane against plane rocket through the window of the place of the cartel meeting, the ship was not too far from the area at the time as it was helping Britain to support Belize against Guatemala. Harry used his radio to contact the boat and ask to speak to the pilot of the plane on the boat which was intended for use against the Belize attackers and had for a short time been set up by Sir Cameron to fly to Colombia and fire the plane to plane rocket as arranged. Harry radioed the pilot so that he could give the Pilot the-longitude and latitude coordinate position of the building and the height of the building and position of the window where the rocket attractor had been placed and therefore which window to aim at. He then returned to his hotel room and waited to see what was going to happen. After a short time, he heard the sound of an aircraft and then a few minutes later saw an explosion occur in the office where the drug cartel meeting had been taking place. The rocket had struck accurately thanks to the attractor as well as the skill of the pilot. And thanks to the effort of Sir Cameron and Harry and the pilot a drug cartel had been removed from the world, Harry was very pleased with the result. He then made his arrangements to leave the country and return home which he did by traveling by train to Panama and there getting a flight to England. Then going to visit Sir Cameron at his office in Baker Street, to find out what his next job would be. Also Harry was becoming concerned about his physical fitness as his work didn't require him to use much energy and muscle strength, so he wanted to discuss with Sir Cameron the possibility of being able to have the free time to do some physical training and running and if possible spend time in Wales at Snowdonia walking and running in mountains. Sir Cameron agreed with him and told him of some weeks he could have time to do his fitness preparation and that he would have these repeated from time to time so as to keep his fitness as his work was very valuable to the Traps organisation and he needed to be both physically and mentally fit to do it properly. Sir Cameron however added he mustn't use the time to carry out private Assassinations as harry had done earlier during his free time from his occupation. Two weeks later Harry was camping near Snowdon on the outskirts of Betws Y Coed and getting ready to walk as quickly as possible to the top of Snowdon. For his first attempt he decided to take the Miners track a straight forward safe track but requiring a good degree of fitness, Harry carried on his back a ruck sac with a good weight of stones in it to make his walk more military and energy using, when he reached the top he was pleased to see there was a café where he could have a coffee before going back down to the camp site where his tent was situated and getting an acholic drink and some dinner in a betws y coed public house, as well as preparing for his next sleep. Back at his tent he changed his clothes and boots and thenwent into the nearest pub for some dinner and a pint of beer and a chat with some of the other customers who were locals, he asked about the different routes to the top of the mountain. And how difficult they were and did he need any climbing equipment to reach the top if he used the more difficult ones. He discovered he had just done just one that was a good energetic walk and if he wanted a difficult one with a little bit of danger, he could try Crib Goch which included a ridge which was very narrow, Like walking along the top of a pitched roof house and needed a good head for heights and a steady nerve to walk along it. Also it would not be sensible to have a ruc sack full of heavy stones because while doing this particular walk a very good sense of balance was needed. There was also the Pyg Track which one had to follow as a start to Crib Goch and for which one could park at Pen Y Pass and set out from there and reach a point where there were two Styles to the left of the track and going to the right at this point led to the Crib Goch start. Harry thanked them for their advice and asked them to show him on his map where each of Crib Goch and The pyg Track were, so that he might use them, they also offered to show him where the miners track was as they said that it was a very even and a good walkers track especially .if he was doing the walks to require good fitness. This being because of it's safe even path and long distance to the top, they did this not knowing he had already done that one, which they did with a little warning about Crib Goch that he should make sure he was wearing non slip boots and not wearing a weighted ruc sack as it could unbalance him. Harry then went back to his tent where he prepared an easy made evening meal for himself before getting ready for bed and settling down for a good night's sleep which he achieved, waking at about 7:30am feeling well rested and eating his breakfast which was raw porridge that he had prepared just before settling for bed, by putting the raw oats in a bowl with some milk and leaving them to soak for the night. Harry liked this breakfast as it was easy to make and the oats in the morning when he ate them were a bit like rice pudding in both taste and texture. Harry got himself dressed and prepared again for another walk up the mountain this time deciding to take Crib Goch, the start of which he found fairly easy although it wasn't a flat track but involved climbing a little and stepping across rocks, the next part the narrow ridge involved walking along a very narrow ridge with a long drop down each side and meant having a good head for heights and very steady feet  while occasionally having to step down a little on one side and lean over to grip the top of the ridge with his hands to keep safe. It was a reasonably quick route to the top and required not much energy. Harry was happy to do it and when he reached the top at about 10;30am he enjoyed a sandwich for an early lunch and a drink in the mountain top restaurant, before returning to the bottom of the mountain taking the miners track as his route and then returning to his tent for about 2:00pm before going for another walk up a different part of the mountains with a local who had offered to support him in his walks. This time across fields, which led higher over a distance and more slowly than the tracks directly to the summit.  He eventually got higher and then reached a cliff with a great beautiful view across the hills and mountains around Snowdon itself, then turning around and following his outward path back, returning to Betws Y Coed for another meeting with the pleasant locals in the pub and a discussion of what he had done so far. Something he enjoyed and then having eaten an evening meal he headed back to his tent and settled down for another good nights sleep feeling he had done a good days exercise  and feeling very satisfied with his day which had been sunny but not too hot, even if it left him a little tired With still four more days of freedom Harry had made an agreement with the local man as to what he could do on some of those days, the man was going to come with him so as to show him the best routes for what Harry had in mind to gain as regards his fitness and ability. They were going towalk up hillsides around Snowden itself which required quite a big use of energy to reach their high points and wonderful views, especially if one had a heavy ruck sac full of stones on one's back, even if these walks were not quite as high as the summit of Snowdon its self.

# Chapter Ten

It was June in the year 2000 and Harry again stood in front of Sir Cameron for another task preparation interview. Sir Cameron said "You probably know about British ship crews who were onboard ships captured by Pirates who were being held hostage in prisons on the land after their Huge unarmed transport vessels and tankers had been captured by the pirates off the African coast in the Indian ocean. Then taken and hidden next to the land.  The crew and any other people who were on board have been badly mistreated by the pirates. Who have demanded large sums of cash

  for the release of the ship, it's crew and any other people on onboard, who were taken hostage when the ship was captured. The pirates  threaten that any person taken hostage on the ship, will be kept, tortured and continually mistreated until they die. Unless the money is paid quickly. The pirates have also whenever possible, been capturing motor yachts of a fair size as these are usually owned by people who are very wealthy and they take the occupants for hostage, expecting to be able to demand large sums of money for their release. The current situation is that all of the captured ships and their crews as well as the wealthy owned motor yachts and those who were on board have all had their ransom paid and as a result have been released and I am sure as a result of this the pirates will be looking to capture more ships and yachts and go through the same  evil activity again. I would like us to put a stop to it if we can."  Harry frowning replied, "Yes Sir, I understand and agree with you  but this is not a job for me as I don't know a great amount about navigating a ship, yes I did manage to bring that motor-powered yacht back from the Mediterranean but I had watched others make that particular journey a few times while I was on board with them and was able to see the coast for a large part of the journey." Sir Cameron then said, "it's not your boating ability that I want but your great weapon ability, your sniper shooting and your clever ideas for dealing with difficult situations. I already have several men who are very used to using moderate sized motor driven yachts and are good at sea navigation, one of them you know very well he is your friend, Frank Norman. I want you to use that motor yacht based at Eastbourne that you captured and turn it into a Q. Boat. Innocent looking yet secretly armed boats have been called Q boats since the first Q boats were used by Britain in world war two. I will supply you with some reasonably sized armaments which you can hide on board, for you and the others to use.so you can go to the area in the Indian ocean where the pirates act and encourage them to come for your boat, thinking it is just some rich person on holiday. Then You can take them by surprise with a successful ambush, It seems at this time they have been using a former transport vessel of their own as a sea base and attacking yachts, with several extremely fast little boats driven by an outboard motor and threatening the yachts with Rifles and machine guns and rocket grenades which they don't actually use to attack but fire just into the sea near the yachts so as to frighten the crews into surrendering but not to damage the yachts or kill the crew members so they have something to ransom. If I arm you with some rocket grenades as well as heavy machine guns and rifles you should be able to win and remove them for good and maybe take over and destroy the transport boat that acts as their sea base." Sounds fine to me said Harry I'll give it a lot of thought and see if I can come up with any ideas to help. Harry now returned home so he could settle down and give the Q. Boat scheme some thought, after a very relaxed walk in the Malvern hills and an evening at home during which he cooked and enjoyed a lovely meal of grilled steak and broad beans with two medium size roast potatoes together with a couple of glasses of a very nice Hungarian red wine called Eger

Bikaver or in English, "Eger Bulls blood." he had decided what his plan should be and that he should go and discuss it with Sir Cameron in the morning after a good night's sleep. Next morning Harry called in to talk to his boss in Sir Cameron's office in Baker street London and found Sir Cameron ready to listen and carry out any suggestions that he made, Harry said, Right Sir Cameron you said the pirates would attack us in small very fast boats with an outboard motor so can you get our technologists to create a large net that floats just below the water which we could tow behind our boat so that it will tangle up the propellers on the attacking boats and bring them to a halt which will allow us to fire at them from a little distance when they are stopped and make sure they cannot get to us and possibly because of their numbers be able to board us even though we are able to begin firing at them from a good distance also a few limpet mines would be a good way to deal with their base ship after we have finished with them. Sir Cameron said I'll see what can be done and try to get you a suitable net. I will also get you a couple of limpet mines to help you deal with the pirates floating base when you have dealt with their attempt to capture your yacht. Two weeks later the 60 foot motor yacht that Harry had previously captured from the weapons smugglers, was ready to leave for the Indian ocean fitted with two Browning .50 cal. heavy machine guns placed on the top of the 20 foot long flying bridge and ready to be fired either forward or sternwards or to port or to starboard and hidden by being surrounded by an armoured bulwark with the armour also hidden behind the original wooden bulwark  and also below the main deck were stored the two limpet mines for hopefully dealing with the Pirates floating base  when the pirates attacking the yacht had already been dealt with, these two mines were placed together with  several rocket propelled grenades some with high explosive anti tank {heat} warheads, while some were stored inside the bridge and ready to be fired through the port, starboard and stern doors. Depending on which direction the Pirate attack came

Also stored on the bridge were the sniper rifles and ammunition for them so that the very good shots on board would be able to aim from the doors of the bridge and pick off the pirates at a good distance, if necessary. In the case of the pirates getting close to the motor yacht and perhaps trying to board it there were also a number of pistols and a number of handheld light machine guns and hand grenades. also the bridge and the lower deck were to be protected by armour plate in case the enemy started firing their AK 47 Kalashnikovs which have a range of at least 300 metres. All the armour plate was placed inside the decks and bridge of the yacht hidden so that it could not be seen from other boats and allow the enemy to think the boat was other than a wealthy persons special play thing. Harry Markham placed in charge led his 5 colleagues chosen by Sir Cameron to inspect the boat at it's berth in Eastbourne. Seeing the weapons and the net as well as how the boat had been adjusted to protect and accommodate six people in reasonable comfort, made them all happy to be doing what they had been detailed to do, in spite of the danger and possibility of death or becoming a hostage being involved in the unknown circumstances of what they would be required to undertake in the next few weeks. Harry took them in the boat a short distance out to sea so they could practice laying out the special net and also so that they could work out the best way to keep or position the weapons so it was quick and easy to get them on deck and ready for use. They also placed the Heavy machine guns in a fixed position on the deck above the flying bridge where they would be good to be fired from if necessary but also where they would be hidden from the view of anyone using a magnifying glass or binoculars to examine the boat from a distance, Harry had asked that three of the other men should be prepared to dress like wealthy women when walking on deck to fool the pirates into thinking they could attack the boat without worrying about any form of defence from its occupants. The three men he asked agreed without any refusal as long as the clothes they needed could be bought by themselves with cash supplied by Sir Cameron, which Harry said he would arrange as soon as possible once they returned to their London offices and he could have the chance to speak again to Sir Cameron.

The special net floated nicely just out of sight under the water and moved away back from the motor yacht as the yacht drove forward, so as long as the enemy speed boats came from behind, they would get their propellers tangled in it as they got about 60 yards close to the yacht. Also, if they were

coming from the side all the yacht had to do was turn in the opposite direction and the net would move behind the yacht and be ready to stop the attack getting close. The major problem with the motor yacht as regards safety was the fact that there had been no armour anywhere on it when built for the previous owners. The smugglers Harry had removed. No armour above the deck or below the deck or on the bridge so any bullets fired at it would penetrate the hull and hit people below deck as well as hitting anyone standing on the deck or navigating the boat on the bridge. Thanks to Harries ability to develop plans for safety and his discussion of matters with Sir Cameron this problem had been solved and only when standing or walking on the deck was there a danger from being fired at from another small boat however in spite of the protective armour plate fitted to the boat it would not have strong enough armour to protect it from shells fired from a heavy gun, say from a destroyer or frigate although this was unlikely to happen in what they were expected to do. The main danger which they would not have much protection from would be the firing of rocket propelled grenades which they had heard were sometimes used by the pirates however they did have some protection by the armour plate newly fitted to the motor yacht and as the pirates were hoping to treat the boat and it's crew as hostages Harry and his colleagues were expecting to be able to deal with all of the pirates before they would wish to fire anything that would wreck the yacht and kill it's crew.

 If for any reason the pirates started firing first, Harry's team would  soon be firing back very strongly themselves, which meant that importantly they would need to keep a good watch and be ready for when the pirates began to approach them and so make their own attack first. Once everything that they wanted had been arranged on the motor yacht, Harry and his five colleagues went out to sea to have a practice at everything including the three chosen for dressing as women, wearing their fancy clothes as well as wearing shoes with heels and looking very much like three wealthy women to anyone looking at them from a distance  Harry had asked some other of their colleagues to follow them in a motor dinghy and to look at the motor yacht using Binoculars to check what they could see  and to test if the net plan and female dress plan would work. To his great pleasure they reported that they couldn't see the heavy machine guns and the boat just looked like a normal expensive motor yacht also the three men disguised as women looked just as they were meant to be, three wealthy women.

 The dinghy had also come onto the net without its crew seeing it and got their outboard engine's propellor tangled in it and had to stop and in order to free it one member had to enter the water with a knife and free the propellor which meant that later Harry would have to have that little part of the net repaired before he could use it again. Which as it had proved it worked successfully didn't bother him too much. Next he had to ask Sir

Cameron to arrange that they could travel down the Suez Canal to the danger area or that they would have to have a destroyer escort to South Africa so they could have the fuel of the yacht topped up ready for when they headed north towards the Arabian ocean. Sir Cameron said, 'I will make arrangements for you to stop at Limassol on the coast of Cyprus for a refuel and then you can continue to the start of the Suez Canal where I'll have made arrangements for you to travel. down it and into the danger area" I will also make arrangements for you to travel back the same way after you have carried out your plan successfully.  A short time later Sir Cameron gave Harry the details of what he had arranged and where he should go to. Then he gave more details to Harry to pass on to the navigator who was going with Harry, these were details of how to get to Limassol on the coast of Cyprus as well as a pass to help with their entrance to the Suez Canal. After receiving this information and the pass, Harry got his team together for another practice session before leaving for Cyprus. Harry satisfied with what he witnessed during the practice, refuelled the yacht a few days later and  together with his colleagues then set off for their journey to the north west of the Indian ocean by way of the Mediterranean, refuelling again at Cyprus, traveling down the Suez canal and into the Arabian sea. and then to the Indian ocean. Shortly after their arrival at their destination one of his colleagues on watch reported seeing a large transport ship stationary in the distance to their port side that looked like it might be the pirates floating base. Harry then encouraged those on watch to keep a good look out for the small speed boats leaving it and asked those dressed as women to walk out onto the deck so they could be seen from the pirate base. He also prepared the rocket grenade launchers in the bridge ready for use and told those who had practiced with the heavy machine guns to get ready for being ordered to hurry up the ladder to the deck above the bridge where the guns were placed, he also made sure all the extra ammunition was readily available in the bridge. after a short time one of those on watch spotted six small speedboats coming towards them each with five men on board. And someone fired several rifle shots from them at Harry's yacht, probably hoping this would make the yacht stop Whereupon Harry ordered the yacht to be turned to the starboard and look as though it was fleeing. The speed boats also turned and started following the yacht, as soon as the speed boats were close enough Harry let them run onto the net before ordering the attack on them which was first carried out by the heavy machine guns. By letting the speed boats enter the area of the net their propellers became jammed and they were unable to flee and their crews were wiped out by the machine guns as well as the boats themselves being wrecked and sunk. Then to Harry's horror one of the lookouts reported two more speed boats coming towards the bows of the yacht. And added it looks like one of the men onboard one of them is aiming a rocket grenade our way, Harry quickly picked up a rifle and shouting to his team start firing toward the boats coming toward the bows, stepping through the side door of the bridge he aimed the rifle at the man holding up the rocket grenade and fired a careful shot which took the man in the head and caused him to drop the rocket grenade meanwhile the heavy machine guns where now taking out the men on board the two speed boats coming towards the bows of the yacht and who had started firing hand held machine pistols at the yacht fortunately only hitting the armoured plating.as Harry's team were all inside the bridge or kneeling below the bulwarks on the deck above the bridge The net was then released and the yacht as quickly as possible moved  away from the dead attackers to make sure that they wouldn't possibly be chased by the large transport ship which was being used  by the pirates as an on the water base. Once a good distance away Harry asked his team to stop as he hoped to be able to return when it was dark and possibly attack the base boat using the limpet mines and so completely remove the pirates from the sea. He thought they could manage this as they had removed thirty or more of the enemy and thought that there might not be so many left on board the base ship. Harry had arranged with Sir Cameron for the supply of the two limpet mines which he as a scuba diver and also capable of diving deep with out scuba equipment was prepared to risk trying to place on the pirate's base ship after dark and blow it up with the rest of the pirates on board, gaining the result of removing all of the remaining pirates. So that they could never capture any more innocent people, torturing them and generally mistreating them as well as making them hostages. That night once it was dark the yacht rode back towards the base ship and stopped far enough away where it wouldn't be seen then Harry launched the yachts small wooden life boat that could be rowed and selected three of his team to row it, then he boarded it with the two mines and they set out to sneak up to the pirate's base ship as quietly as possible, then when a few feet away Harry who was naked except for a pair of swimming trunks slipped very quietly into the water with one of the mines which were quite heavy to carry but have a slight buoyancy when in water to make them easier to handle and he swam to the ship before diving underwater and placing the mine quietly on the hull of the ship, he then returned and took the other mine which he also quickly and quietly placed on other side hull of the ship and returned to board the rowing boat with his colleagues and encouraged them to row as quickly and as quietly away as they could before the mines were set off by their time fuses ,after they had rowed for about fifteen minutes and were a good distance from the ship, they heard an explosion quickly followed by another one and knew that their plan had worked and the pirates had been removed completely. Once they had returned to the yacht Harry thanked all of his team members and said how pleased he was with the great job they had done and how much congratulations they would each receive from Sir Cameron. With the job finished the team headed for the Suez Canal to return to the Mediterranean to again visit Limassol on the coast of Cyprus in order to refuel and thanks to Sir Cameron's arrangement, they had no problems with the journey back and went to Limassol in Cyprus and refuelled the yacht then headed back to Eastbourne and the yachts berth place. In five more weeks, they were again meeting Sir Cameron and being thanked and congratulated. From Sir Cameron's point of view because of the major effort they had made and the possible danger involved, they deserved a medal  for what they had done but because of the secrecy of what they did they couldn't get one, otherwise what the organisation did would become known to everyone in the UK. And possibly other countries and then they would become targets for complaint and possibly terrorism against themselves, the end result being they would no longer be able to do the work they had been doing in removing lots of evil people from society and as a result, saving many innocent lives.

# Chapter Eleven

Fourteen year old Margaret Timbola who lived in  a village in Oxfordshire was having a hard time with her parents who like all good parents were worried about keeping her safe from county line drug peddlers or a possible rape so kept refusing to let her go out really late at night with her school friends even though they were all very nice sensible young girls, or stay with them at weekends, they also were letting her have very little money as only her father worked  and they were quite poor.  This had caused Margaret to take on a part time job working for a nearby newspaper shop for which she delivered daily newspapers and weekly magazines which meant she had little free time in the afternoons to spend with her friends.

Margaret decided to leave home and go to London and hope to find a job there and  hopefully a nice place to live. Her best friend Susan who she told what she was going to do and who had originally lived in Enfield a very nice part of North London. warned her to be very careful when she arrived at the London Paddington station following her train journey. Susan told Margaret not to allow herself to be taken for foolish by some young man and enticed into going  to stay with him as often when this happened, nice as the young man might seem he could be working for a group of paedophiles and could force Margaret to become available to a large number of older men. Margaret listened carefully to what her friend Susan was telling her and decided to take care as warned.

Arriving at Paddington, Margaret sat on a seat in the station and when approached by any male did as her friend had told her to do which was get up and go into the restaurant and talk to a waiter so that should she need help it would be readily available and the young man would probably go away somewhere else.

After several male approaches Margaret was approached by what she assumed was a very pleasant elderly woman who turned out to be in her forties. Margaret after a chat with her and explaining how she had run away from home was invited to come with the woman who offered her some accommodation saying she was a widow and was very lonely and in need of some nice company. Margaret having been approached by several young boys and having to keep going into the restaurant for safety and starting to feel frightened, accepted her kind offer and they left the station together and went to a flat about a half hours walk from the station, the woman showing her friendship offered to carry one of Margaret's clothes bags to give her arm a little rest, Margaret pleased to have met such a caring person said, "yes please." and gave her one of her bags to carry, Once settled in the woman's flat, Margaret enjoyed a delicious homemade piece of fruit cake and a nice cup of tea.

The woman showed Margaret a bedroom with a nice single bed in it, which was to be Margaret's for as long as she stayed in the flat. As the weeks and months went on the woman provided Margaret with some delicious homemade meals and on several occasssions took her out in the evening to restaurants and a few evenings to discos where Margaret made more friends both male and female. The woman also frequently cuddled Margaret after they had been out and when they returned to the flat and then gave her a few small drinks of wine both of which Margaret enjoyed. After some more time the woman became even more loving and occasionally kissed Margaret on the lips and as winter approached and the flat got a bit colder as there wasn't any central heating just an electric fire in the Lounge and another in what was used as the dining room, the woman suggested that Margaret should join her in her double bed each night to keep them both warm, which Margaret was happy to do.  Mary which Margaret had learned was the woman's name, now began to cuddle a lot more. Stroking Margaret's young breasts and inviting Margaret to stroke hers,

The cuddling developed after some time to a form of love making which both seemed to enjoy very much. Margaret was also introduced to cannabis smoking as each day progressed which she also enjoyed. Not realising that she could be doing harm to herself.

After a little more time and now after Margaret's fifteenth birthday, Mary found Margaret a job as an assistant in a Nearby shop which sold books and this enabled her to earn some money for herself. First Mary had told Margaret that she must keep it secret, all the things they were doing together. Especially the bedtime activities and the cannabis smoking, Margaret remembering that her parents had warned her about the county line smugglers and the illegal side of drugs agreed and was always careful when in conversation with others never to mention what she was involved in.  One day when it rained very heavily Margaret returned from work early as the shop had become very wet inside and had closed early, when she arrived back at Mary's flat, to her surprize there were two men in the flat who looked like they were from India or Pakistan. Mary introduced them and it turned out they were not from India or Pakistan but from somewhere in the North African deserts, Mary also asked why Margaret was home early and Margaret explained. The two men seemed very angry at Margaret's arrival. Then Mary asked Margaret to go to her bedroom and leave her to speak to the two men on her own.
As Margaret entered her bedroom she heard Mary say, "of course I'll do as you ask me you know I'm already a follower of your beliefs even if I break a few of them occasionally due to my previous habits." After about another half hour the two men left and Mary called Margaret back to the lounge. There for them to

have a pleasant evening together. One morning a week later Mary said to Margaret, "I have a favour I want you to do for me, I want you to make a delivery for me of a case of drugs to a young man who is a friend of mine. I want them delivered in a tricky secret way which I'll explain to you this afternoon."

"Fine," said Margaret, "you have done so much for me, I'll be pleased to do it". That afternoon Mary explained to Margaret, "I want you to take this red suitcase and board a train to Oxford from Paddington, I'll help you carry it to the station, when on the train leave the case in the gap behind your seat, you must not open the case until the train is leaving the station because if what is in it is smelt by anyone who recognises it, then they may try to steal it or leave the train and report you to the police as a County line drug peddler but once you are on the moving train then it Should be safe for you to check what is in it before giving it to my friend Phil, also don't have a conversation with Phil when he comes to collect it, he will quietly say, thank you Margaret and also ask you to thank Mary for her gift. so you will know it is the right young man and don't need to worry about it" at this point you should open the case and show him what is in it. After making sure Margaret understood what to do on the train. For the rest of the day Mary's behaviour was as usual an Afternoon of shopping. Later followed by a visit to a restaurant for a lovely evening meal and then back home in time for bed. A few days later Mary said to Margaret, "I would like you to make my delivery today please, here are all the things you need and what to do. Mary gave Margaret a return ticket from Paddington to Reading warning her that the young man would approach her about 15 minutes after the train left the station at Paddington and to make sure the case was convenient to be opened and handed over to the young man. Mary now waited till Margaret was ready to leave and then left with her to take her to the station and to Help her carry the case. Shortly before arriving at the station Mary handed the case over to Margaret and left her to enter the station on her own and board the great Western railway train going to Reading, for which she had the ticket. What Margaret didn't know was the case contained a bomb and when she opened the case to check the contents in preparation for showing the contents to the young man then the bomb would explode killing her, the young man and many others on the train as well as wrecking the train. After the train was wrecked the police carried out a very intensive search and scientific examination of everything possible as well as questioning everyone back at Paddington station to see what they could find out and prove. They wanted to check any camera results from the station to see if anyone could be seen carrying the bomb case. Firstly they found out from the technicians helping them that the fuse had been set off by the opening of the case and also from the tiny bits spread around that the bomb had been contained in a red case. Which directed them to Margaret but not the young man who was still some distance from the bomb when Margaret opened it, getting ready to show him but still close enough to be killed by it. Taking samples of the wrecked bodies and checking the DNA they found some was the same as that of the missing Margaret Timbola that they had been trying to find for quite some time since her disappearance which had been reported to the police by her parents who had given the police photographs of Margaret to help them find her. The police thinking that she possibly had travelled to Paddington when she disappeared from home began looking at films taken of the station previously, knowing when she had disappeared from home ,made it easier to know which films to look at, they saw Margaret being spoken to by a number of young men and then by a strange woman about the time she had gone missing and saw a film of her and the woman leaving the station together. They also saw pictures of Margaret and the woman coming into the station on the day of the explosion with

Margaret carrying a red case and the scientific bomb experts had said from the wreckage found around where the bomb had exploded that there was  indication it had probably been in a red case, so now the police set out to find who the strange woman was that had taken the young girl out of the station some weeks earlier and if she had any connections with terrorists. After a few weeks of research and using the CCTV pictures. They found out who she was and where she lived, this then led to people who were her neighbours, when questioned mentioning about the arrival of a new young girl in her flat at about the day Margaret had disappeared from home, they also mentioned the visits to the flat in the recent couple of weeks by a number of men with darker than normal skin. The police now questioned Mary who admitted Looking after Margaret but denying any knowledge of Margaret knowing about bombs or having any connections with terrorists. When asked about  the visits by the two  darker skinned men she said they were just people they had met whilst out shopping and they had taken a liking to Margaret.  Mary had warned her not to get involved with them in case they were after making her into a sex plaything. The police asked some specific questions about bombs and Mary denied any knowledge of bombs or ever having anything to do with them or any form of terrorism. The police ended it at that and left the flat with the intensions of keeping a watch on the flat and those who visited it. The result of this was that they became very aware that there was a connection between Mary and some known terrorist supporters, Information that eventually ended up being passed to Sir Cameron who passed it on to Harry and several other members of his team. Harry took it upon himself to remove Mary and set about making a plan that would make it seem like a non political murder. Firstly he visited Mary, checking first that the police had stopped watching her flat, he told her he was representing Margaret's parents who the police had told about Mary and were very grateful  how she had looked after their daughter when she first came to London and had kept her away from any evil people until the bomb incident when Margaret was probably returning home. He then offered to take her to meet Margaret's parents who he said were waiting in their home near chipping Norton. Mary agreed to come if she could ring the police first and check on who Harry was. The police knowing Harry was employed by the Government in a type of policing organisation, replied that it would be fine and safe and she should go ahead. Harry said he would take her by rail to Charlbury where his car was parked and then to a House near Chipping Norton where she would meet Margaret's parents. To do this they went to Paddington station. Harry having already checked that the wrecked train would have been moved and the track repaired and back in good order again. He was fortunate, everything was back to normal and he would be able to carry out his plan and board a train with Mary and travel to where his car was parked. In Charlbury,. Which They did and then entered the car and headed back towards Chipping Norton, about half way there Harry pulled onto a road leading to Kingham and his house. He drove in through his main gate and up to the building . Asked Mary to stay in the car and opened his garage doors then returned to the car and drove in, he helped Mary get out of the car and led her into his lounge saying to her, "please sit here while I make you a cup of tea and contact Margaret's parents who would like to meet you." Mary replied, "I hope they are not blaming me for what happened to her." Harry smiled at her and said, "no they think it was something to do with Terrorists who give her the red case to carry for them without her knowing what was inside it." That evening Harry was joined by three more of his colleagues and all four of them took Mary down to the cellar in the house and told her they wanted to know who the dark skinned men were who had visited her and why. Mary gave no answer and Harry said, Mary we want an accurate answer now or we will make things very difficult for you in the next few minutes and with that two of the others grabbed her by the arms and tied them behind her back with a wide sticky tape. Then another one of them who was smoking a cigarette threatened to press it into her cheek if she didn't answer the questions they were about to ask her. They then went on to question her about the whole business and wither the young girl knew what was going to happen and why such a young girl brought up in the British countryside would want to commit suicide as well as killing many other innocents in such a terrorist way. Mary now sobbing told them the two dark skinned men had come to speak to her because they were interested in buying her former husband's business and she was pleased to sell it to them as she knew little about what was required to do in it and wasn't capable of running it, the business was called Marsh & Ross and the two men were going to continue to use that name. as they continued to run the same business which made and sold and rented movable railings to the police and other government organisations that used them to temporally protect areas that large numbers of people were starting to approach.

Having got the information they wanted from Mary they decided she had known about the bomb and been helping terrorists and should be killed which they did  by knocking her out and suffocating her, After this they placed her in the boot of Harry's car under several old coats so that she was hidden,  Harry then set out with his colleagues for his plane at the nearby private airfield where he kept it. On arrival he showed his pass to the gate guard who waved him through and he  drove straight to his plane with the other members of his team one of whom was willing to help him by coming with him on the flight and dropping the body into the Atlantic  as Harry flew the plane. Having travelled late in the day with his colleagues to where his plane was stationed and It had  now become dark, they were able to carry Mary's body from the boot of the car without it being seen by anyone  and put it into the plane,  Harry then together with his colleagues returned to his house where he rang Sir Cameron and asked him to make Harry's usual flight plan for 10:00am the next morning. Then following  a good night's sleep and a nice typical English breakfast of eggs and bacon, Harry returned to the private airfield with the one of his colleagues who had agreed to fly with him and together they took off and flew west to the Irish sea and then headed North and around the top of Northern Ireland until the plane was over the Atlantic, at which point he turned west again and headed well out towards America and after about an hour he asked his colleague to drop the body which had been attached to weights out, so it would fall into the water and sink deep, far enough across the Atlantic at a spot where hopefully it would be eaten by fish and never  be found again. That done he turned back landing at the private airfield where he kept his plane and driving with his colleague back to his home near the village of Kingham. Where they both had a meal and settled down with a glass of wine with the others who had stayed there having spent the previous night with Harry before each going to bed in his house and enjoying a peaceful night's sleep. Next morning they too had enjoyed a nice traditional English breakfast of eggs and bacon supplied by Harry. When Harry and his helping Colleague arrived back, they all went off   together to see Sir Cameron and Harry explained what he had done. And said he could provide the names and addresses of the two men involved in visiting Marys flat and if Sir Cameron wanted they could be removed or just reported to the police but he thought   it best if they were removed as the police would find it difficult to prove that they were involved in the bombing as well as the woman and the probably innocent young girl. He also explained to Sir Cameron about them taking over the movable railings business and told Sir Cameron about his thoughts on the matter, he explained that he thought that they were probably going to insert explosives with a radio fired fuse into the hollow pipe work used to make the railings and fire them when some important people or several police or military where nearby therefore the sooner they were removed the better and Harry and his colleagues were just waiting for Sir Cameron to give them the go ahead

Although the woman and the girl didn't have the knowhow to make such a bomb as the one involved in the train explosion and the girl thought the case just contained something, not exactly innocent but the same as she had become used to enjoying in the evenings with Mary, as a present for another young man who was supposed to be a friend of Mary the woman who knew exactly what the case contained and what would set it off, all this Harry and his colleagues had discovered from the very forceful questioning of Mary the woman, who knew what was going to happen and had just made use of the innocent young girl.

Now with Sir Cameron's permission they were sorting out a plan to secretly remove the two terrorists who had set up the bomb and now were probably making many more in the movable railings they produced. To get to know the two men and see what they looked like Harry and one of his colleagues went to the business the two men had bought from Mary and asked if they could rent some mobile fence as they were helping a man who was living in Cirencester and about to have a grand fair sales event for those who did past times skilled work, for example spinning and weaving or carpentry making classic furniture. They said that some tempory fencing was needed to keep vehicles limited to certain routes and parking spaces as well as keeping the people visiting by walking, limited to tracks where their tickets could be checked so they would all have to pay to visit the fair. The two men replied, "sorry but we only supply our goods to police or local Government's as we have limited supplies and don't want to upset those who have made most use of this business by not being able to supply them with the equipment that is often very important for them. Harry now that he knew the appearance of the two men accepted their refusal politely as he would want to make further contact with them when he was ready to remove them permanently. His friend while he had been talking to the two men and had gained their attention had managed to get a photo of each of them to give to Sir Cameron to pass to other members of the Traps organisation. So that as needed, a watch could be kept on them.

A few days later Harry asked Sir Cameron to check if the police were using any of the mobile fencing and if so could it be borrowed by Sir Cameron without telling them why and checked to see if it contained any explosives. This was done and it turned out to be a fact that it did contain explosives. Then Harry discovered some of the mobile barricades were being used at the entrance to Downing street, so he went there immediately to check where they had come from because if they were the explosive ones then a large crowd of people would be killed if they exploded, also depending on the circumstances if they were to explode just as the PM was driving into the street and had stopped while the street gates where opened then the PM would also be killed.  A few days later Harry and a couple of his colleagues again went to have a look at the entrance to Downing street as they looked they saw that the gates were closed and a car drove up and stopped  probably with the PM in it and then Harry having moved away towards where he had seen one of the two suspects saw the man  standing about fifty yards from the entrance and watched him take a radio out of his pocket, Harry was shocked and thought gosh he is going to set off a bomb  and we must stop him. With that thought in his mind Harry hurried towards the man and came up behind the suspect and hit him on the hand with a club knocking the radio from his hand before he could set the bomb off then Harry took out his pistol and ordered the man to come with him or he would shoot him there and then. The man said, "what have I done wrong that you are threatening me, in a minute I am going to yell to the police for help." Harry had by this time been joined by his two colleagues and he took his club out again and hit the suspect on the head knocking him out. As he fell his two colleagues caught him and together with Harry began to carry him away to their car where they put him in the boot then tied his ankles together and also his hands with the usual broad tape that Harry carried in his car After doing this Harry went back to the entrance to Downing Street and spoke to the police telling them who he worked for and that the police must check the tempory barricades for explosives. The police were from across the road at Scotland yard the London cosmopolitan police station where Harry and his colleagues had spoken to the police earlier that day so the police knew what was being explained to them and told Harry they would take some of the tempory barricade away and check it for explosives and then if they found it was affected they would replace the remainder with some which they knew was safe and go to the business and arrest the two new owners. Harry said to them don't worry about going to see the new owners my comrades and I will deal with them as we are trained to do and in a way that they won't cause anymore trouble for anyone. The police knowing who they worked for said OK go ahead as quickly as you can, you will save us a lot of work trying to get them to court and into prison quickly and without any fuss and then psycho analysts trying to teach them to stop being terrorists before they are eventually released.

Having removed any interference from the police Harry and his comrades took the man they had captured to Harry's house and shot him so Harry could take him over the Atlantic and drop his body in to the water then they went back to the business buildings they had visited before and meeting the other thug shot him as well and took his body to join the other one at Harry's house so both could be weighted so they would sink when dropped together by Harry and one of his colleagues in the Atlantic. Which Harry did the following day with the help of one of his colleagues,  who had been involved in the killing of the two terrorists  and was willing to help to make the dead bodies disappear by pushing them out of the plane as Harry flew over the Atlantic ocean having asked Sir Cameron as usual to prepare a flight plan for him.

# Chapter Twelve

It was 8<sup>th</sup>of May 1980 in Australia and Harry Markham at that time having just been annoyed as a member of the Australian SAS at having to help to put out forest fires instead of using his Military skills to take Military action against some of Australia's enemies. Resigned from being a member of the Australian SAS and decided to go to England to live. Harry had just been listening to a television news program the night before  which had encouraged him to decide to leave for England.   This program included the story about the ending of the siege of the Iranian embassy in London. Since leaving Australia he had been working in Britain for some time for an antiterrorist organisation called Terrorist Raiders Assassination Provider Selection or "TRAPS" for short.  Harry had now come to see Sir Cameron Bradley-Stuart the leader of the TRAPS organisation to ask why some of his colleagues who were in the traps organisation at the time of the Guerrilla raid on the Iranian Embassy had happened before he joined TRAPS. Hadn't been asked to carry out the Iranian Embassy rescue instead of the SAS. Sir Cameron replied, the SAS were chosen to carry out the rescue because they are trained to work as a team.  Team workers being best for success in cases like that and the SAS are also trained in the use of the equipment that would have been needed to enable the entrance to the Embassy to take place in an unexpected way as well as quickly and  as a result allow the rescue to take place as safely as possible for the hostages. Apart from yourself no others working here have been SAS trained so best if we stick to our own individual and secret type of methods of dealing with terrorism. Which are intended to prevent others from becoming encouraged to hate Britain and so become terrorists themselves. That is why we act secretly to remove terrorists completely, so they cannot have future opportunities to carry out their terrorist killings and destruction and so no one else knows what happened and are encouraged to join the terrorist organisation and so make it bigger. The results of the embassy siege and it's brilliant solution by the SAS caused something that we wouldn't want to happen as we are a secret organisation and wish to remain so. The results showed what a success the SAS had been in dealing with it and then as well as making them known to everybody in Britain, they became world known. Changing from being a semi-secret regiment known about by very few people. This also demonstrated to the world the possible toughness the British government would use and the future British attitude towards hostage takers and terrorists because like we do, they even removed permanently, most of the guerrillas involved in the hostage taking.

The **Iranian Embassy siege** took place from 30th April to 5th May 1980. When six armed guerrillas stormed the Iranian Embassy in Prince's Gate at South Kensington, London. The gunmen, representing Iranian Arabs seeking for the sovereignty of Khuzestan Province, took twenty six people hostage. Including embassy staff, and several others, some of whom were visitors to the Embassy as well as the police officer who was also taken hostage while on guard duty at the embassy. The hostage takers demanded the freedom of prisoners in Khuzestan and their own safe passage out of the United Kingdom. The British government quickly decided that safe passage would not be granted which had been its normal reaction in the past to terrorists taking hostages and making demands on theUKgovernment. Consequently a siege was begun, Subsequently, the experienced and highly trained British police negotiators who arrived together with armed police officers to stop the guerrillas escaping were able to gain the release of five hostages in exchange for minor concessions, such as allowing broadcasting on BBC and world television of the hostage-takers' demands on

Britain and Iran, which was part of the reason Harry whilst living in Australia had come to gain an interest about what was happening. Before he had watched the later Television News program about what the SAS had done.

By the sixth day of the siege the gunmen were becoming fed up that their demands were not being met. They therefore killed a hostage and tossed the dead body out of the embassy. The Special Air Service  now known as the (SAS) a special forces British military regiment which had  been greatly developed to deal with such problems since they were first created and started to fight against the Germans in north Africa during the second world war. Were asked to rescue the remaining hostages, The rescue was called Operation "Nimrod." To rescue the remaining hostages they abseiled from the roof of the embassy and forced entry to the embassy by crashing through the upper windows into the room where the terrorists had kept the hostages. During their very quick and unusual entrance and attack lasting just over 15 minutes they rescued all but one of the remaining hostages and killed five of the six hostage-takers.  The one remaining guerrilla was imprisoned in England for twenty seven years in normal prisons before being returned to his own country.

The SAS received no accusations of doing anything wrong for the killing of the other guerrillas or the unfortunate Hostage who was killed by the guerrillas during the rescue or for the other hostage who was wounded during the rescue, also one of the SAS was wounded during the rescue, being shot by the hostage takers.

Harry Having  heard the story remembered it and now having discussed it with Sir Cameron, and listened to Sir Cameron's comments. Realised that maybe he would have been better to have joined the British SAS instead of TRAPS although he was still very satisfied with most of the work he had done under the orders of Sir Cameron. Which had involved  the removal of several terrorists as well as  terrorist encouragers, financiers, supporters and some drug smugglers and their suppliers,  having already taken out these evil people and therefore had probably saved a good number of innocent lives as a result.

Harry now decided that he must keep his personal fitness in very good order in case he did decide to try and join the British SAS. He also thought he ought to use more often the shooting club he had joined to keep his shooting ability at it's best, he also went to an airfield near Peterborough where they taught people parachuting, he showed them his reports from his previous jumps with the Selous Scouts and at Peterborough was able therefore, after some retraining in the right way to leave the plane and how to land properly and control and steer a parachute,  to make three jumps using a fixed cable. His hope  in doing this was that if he did them well and then gained more good reports on his ability and producing the reports alongside his previous ones he would be offered the opportunity of a freefall jump. Which he could add to the skills and abilities that he could already was able to offer the SAS. To help him gain a place with them, should he later decide he wanted to join them. He made his three jumps very successfully and was given good reports and a few days afterwards was allowed to make his first free fall jump, he also received a good report on it and was thereafter free to make all of his jumps as free jumps, which he began to do a week later, after having checked with Sir Cameron that he wasn't needed to remove any terrorists and could have the free time which Sir Cameron said was fine and he could go ahead and make the jumps. Which Harry did releasing the chute initially just after he had left the plane and finally making one where he was able to fall for a long way through the air before releasing the chute. The plane took him to twelve thousand feet high, before he jumped and he then released the parachute after twenty seconds which meant a free fall or sky dive  as it is usually called, of four thousand feet which Harry rather enjoyed and thought he would like to do again some other time as the effort and initial stress involved, even though he enjoyed the free fall, left him a little tired to try another without a period of rest. Cnsequently he left the air field and returned home but with the thought that he would have another go as soon as possible. Which would have to be when he next had enough freedom from his work tasks to have time to do it. And had saved enough money to afford it, as parachuting wasn't the cheapest of sports.

# Chapter Thirteen

It was now quite a few months since Harry had carried out the fencing coaching and became a friend of Rima, then went to Syria and assassinated her father. He was now wondering how this would have affected her and if she still was getting enough income to enable her to continue studying at Oxford. Harry thought about what he had done to her by the assassination and decided to go to the fencing club and check if she was still going to it and if so, speak to her and show friendship again then find out how she was coping. The next night the fencing club was running, Harry parked up the street a little way and went to see what was happening at the club. He went in and spoke to Dennis the coach first of all and asked him if Rima was still attending as he hadn't seen her, Dennis said yes she was still attending and was here tonight you just haven't recognised her as she is wearing her protective fencing mask, she is fencing just across the hall from where we are standing now. She has been coming to the club but has shown little enthusiasm and at times has been sitting crying instead of taking part. A little later after Rima finished fencing against the other male fencer, Harry approached her and they fenced each other for a short time until Rima said, "I have done enough for tonight and want to return home." Harry replied, Fine would you like a lift as I will be going soon." "Oh! Yes please," said Rima I would enjoy a talk and a ride in a car with you again." A short time later, both having taken off their fencing clothing they met again and Harry said, "follow me, my car is just up the street a short distance." they went up to Harry's car and Rima put her fencing bag on the back seats where Harry also put his. Then both getting into the front of the car, Rima helped by Harry onto the front passenger seat and Harry then going round to the drivers side and sitting on the driving seat, starting the engine and setting out towards Woodstock where Rima was living in a flat in Union street, which was on Harrys way home, after a journey in which Rima didn't talk but appeared to be crying and had taken out a handkerchief and was wiping her eyes from time to time, they arrived at Woodstock and turned down to Union street

Harry stopped where he had stopped when he had brought Rima to her flat before and Rima said, "before we get out would you agree to join me for a coffee or maybe a cup of tea." Harry in a pleasant voice said, " I would really enjoy that, it is very kind of you." They both got out of the car. Rima collecting her bag off the back seat and Harry offering to carry it for her. Together with Rima leading they went into her flat. Rima went into the kitchen while Harry sat on the sofa, in only about five minutes Rima returned with a tray on which there were two cups of coffee and a plate of mixed biscuits  which she put down on the coffee table in front of the sofa where Harry was sitting and then sat beside Him. Harry noticed that Rima had been crying again, her eyes were a bit inflamed looking and her cheeks wet. He said to Rima,"Rima thank you for the coffee can you tell me what it is that is upsetting you?" Rima burst into tears and said, "My father has been murdered by terrorists in Syria and now I am an orphan, my mother is also dead. I never really knew  her because she and my father never married or lived together after I was born.  Shortly after I was born my father who fortunately had finished his degree, discovered his father who was in his late seventies had died. This resulted in my father having to leave Britain to take over his father's business. My mother then returned to her family in Ireland and I was taken by my father to Syria where I lived with him in Damascus until I was old enough and able to return to study in Britain at a public school here in Oxford and then taking my A levels and qualifying to have a place at Oxford University for which I was thrilled to apply for. Then following my success at the interview each person must satisfy before being offered their place, I was able to attend.  Since then

I have learned from a letter sent to my father by my mother's family telling him that she was killed some years ago by a bomb explosion in a shop in Belfast. By having kept the company of my father and coming to study in Oxford I was helped to get over the very bad news as I had not really known my mother except as a very small baby. That explosion was set off by Terrorists as well and my heart is broken now and I am nearly at a loss to know what to do with my life". This tale really upset Harry who from his own experience knew just how she must be feeling. He put his arm around her and gave her a cuddle thinking to himself that he too was not much better than a terrorist and it was time he changed and began to try and become a more normal person. Rima leaned against him and kissed his cheek making Harry feel even worse at what he had done even though he knew her father had financed terrorists who had probably been responsible for many deaths themselves, causing vast amounts of unhappiness and now knowing Rima's innocent mother had been killed by terrorists. He told Rima how sorry he was for her and said from personal experience he knew exactly how she was feeling as something similar had happened to him and he explained to her about the terrible killing of all of his family when he lived in Rhodesia. He also asked her how she was managing financially, and if she needed any help. Rima still sobbing replied, "I am fine as regards money it is loneliness which is having a bad effect on me, my father had already paid for the university studies and he had arranged for me to have a bank account with 800,000 British pounds in it and after he was killed I have been sent more cash to my bank account from his brother who was given most of what my father had left of the large amount of money he got when he sold his business. I now have a million British pounds in my account. This flat was where my mother lived when she studied here, and the rent is quite reasonable. Fortunately I decided to study teaching when I completed my degree which was in mathematics and I should have my teaching certificate in a few weeks so I should be able to find a good job when I have finished." Harry now feeling very upset and beginning to regret what he had done, said, "."I will come and visit you as often as you wish and support you when I can." He also knew he had to make sure that Rima never found out what his job was and how he might have been responsible for her father's death, maybe it was time he Joined the SAS as he had initially wished to do. Thinking about making a change to his life Harry wondered how his resignation would be taken by Sir Cameron and also what he must do if he wanted to join the SAS and if he did join them would he really be changing his murderous life, after all in the attack on the Islamic embassy when it was held by hostage taking Guerrillas the SAS had needed to kill all of the hostage takers to succeed in rescuing the hostages. He decided he would discuss everything with his father's brother first. Harry now considered his friendship with Rima which had become true love on his part and wondered if the little bit of cuddling he had carried out with her could be extended if he married her and that marrying her would enable him to look after her and see she had a decent life, in spite of what he had done to her father, so at the first suitable opportunity he would ask her if she would marry him. He was already feeling very loving of her and hoped she also felt loving of him. Before leaving to return home and after Rima while still sitting beside him put her arms around Harry again and gave him another cuddle with a kiss on the cheek followed by Harry kissing her on the lips and then asking her if she would like to marry him and getting the answer, "yes of course I would you have been so nice and kind to me, both at the fencing club and now since I have been so upset with the loss of my father." Harry gave her another gentle squeeze and said, "Shall I allow you to make the arrangements or would you like me to do it?" Rima replied, "yes please you probably understand what to do better than I will." "Fine," said Harry, "would you like to be married in a church or have a civil wedding in a registry office?" Rima replied, "I think a registry office would be best as I was brought up as a Member of Islam." Right," said Harry, "Do you have an English passport as you were born in England and your mother was from Northern Ireland? If you do, could I borrow it to take to the registry office as they will want to see it?" "Yes," replied Rima and got up and went and fetched her passport which she gave to Harry who said, "thank you

I will make the arrangements and I look forward to taking you to my house near Kingham which is a very nice village to live in or in my case live near, there are several good schools in the area both primary and secondary so when you have your teaching qualification you should be able to get some nice employment if you would like to work in the area of the village" Rima smiled and seemed to be feeling a lot better than when Harry had first met with her again. Harry now decided to return home and asked Rima if she would like to come with him so that she would have company However Rima said, "no unless Harry would be able to take her by car to oxford each day so she could get her studies completed." Harry not knowing what work he would in future be doing had to answer, "sorry but I don't know if I would have the free time to be able to guarantee that I would be in a position for to do that for you every day." So to help with giving you good company I will visit you here whenever I can until we are married and you have finished your course. Harry was concerned as to what sort of job he could get if he stopped working for the TRAPS organisation and didn't join the SAS however he also thought that if he joined the SAS he wouldn't be able to be a good husband to Rima as he probably would end up leaving her on her own for very long periods by having to carry out attacks in foreign countries such as had happened in the Falkland's not so long ago. He would also have to spend time away from home on training and exercises to develop the required abilities and skills required of all members of the SAS or worst of all the possibility of him being killed by some enemy and again bringing a large amount of upset to Rima. Then Harry thought of his bank manager friend Richard Welldean who he had helped when his daughter was murdered by the couple who tried to carry out a hold up of his bank and during it shot a round into the ceiling and killed his daughter who was sitting in his office as he had brought her with himself for a visit to the bank and have the opportunity to spend the morning with her father playing games etc. Harry thought I'll ask Richard as soon as possible if he could offer me a permanent job sometime in the next six months. After leaving Rima and returning to his own home Harry rang Richard Welldean the bank manager and arranged to meet him the next morning before he went to London as usual to meet Sir Cameron and discuss his next terrorist removal task.

Next morning about 8:00am Harry met Richard at his house and after a friendly chat with him arranged to visit him in his office in the late afternoon, Harry then set off to visit Sir Cameron at the TRAPS organisation office in Baker street. Arriving about 11"00am he sat down in Sir Cameron's office in front of Sir Cameron and began to talk about his wish to give up his job. Sir Cameron to his surprise was quite keen on the idea and then explained why. The government had changed and he felt the TRAPS organisation would be disbanded as its activities were not very British in their nature and the new government wouldn't wish to allow them any longer so the TRAPS organisation would return to its original tasks these being studies of terrorism and it's causes. Instead of being an assassination organisation for the removal of terrorists and other evil wreckers of innocent people's lives, such as drug smugglers and dealers, weapon smugglers and paedophiles. Harry agreed with Sir Cameron's thoughts and retired finally from the organisation asking Sir

Cameron what the other members of the Organisation would do when they had to resign saying like me they won't be suited to chatting to evil people and doing nothing physical to them to prevent their bad behaviour. Sir Cameron then told him to leave and gave him a reference saying he had been very good at his work and several other good things such as how good Harry was at organising things and how honest he had been but without actually mentioning what his job had been and suggested Harry find himself another job as soon as he could. He also told Harry that those of his colleagues who had been involved In the actual assassinating part of the organisation would be recommended by and given a reference from Sir Cameron to help them join the army, the navy or the RAF, whichever they preferred and those involved in the technical side of things would receive a good reference just as he had said he would give to Harry and hopefully find jobs involving their technical knowledge. Possibly with the Army, Navy or Airforce or other businesses where their ability would prove useful. Sir Cameron had because of the nature of Harry's work, previously provided Harry with a proper English passport as well as the artificial South African one. The English Passport would now help Harry to get married in England and find another job. Harry then returned to Chipping Norton where His friend Richard Welldean was a bank manager and went into the bank and up to the manager's office where he was able to have a conversation with Richard as previously arranged that morning and sitting down before the desk asked if he could have a job as a bank assistant and showed him the reference from Sir Cameron and his English passport, Richard out of friendship and impressed by the reference Said, "he didn't have any spare jobs at present but as soon as he did he would offer one to Harry which he expected to be in the next year or so as one of his assistants was approaching their sixty fourth birthday and would probably be retiring when they reached sixty five." Harry said thank you and feeling very relieved that he would have some free time to enable him to enjoy some traveling fun with Rima after he married her and still have a good job to look forward to. He set about arranging his wedding with Rima in the nearest registry office to where he and Rima lived. Harry decided Banbury would be the best place and also somewhere they could have a little party afterwards with a few friends if they wanted to.

The next day Harry made his way to Banbury and went to the registry office where they told him he had to make the arrangement twenty eight days before the day it could take place and then he had to complete the wedding within six months of the date he made the arrangement on and in the registry office he chose. Learning this Harry made the arrangements for the wedding to take place in five weeks time on a Saturday mid-morning, to allow for the fact that Rima was still studying during the week, then he went to visit Rima that evening and told her what he had done and asked if she would like a little party afterwards with a few friends and could she let Harry know as soon as possible and he would arrange that as well. Rima said the day chosen was very good as it was on a Saturday so she would be free from her studies and able to attend with ease and she would let Harry know if any of her friends would be coming and ask him to arrange a small party for afterwards. Then she said of course we won't be going anywhere for a honeymoon as I will have to return to my studies on the Monday that follows and Harry replied you can have a honeymoon with me in Kingham for a couple of days  and later when you have finished your course and have started work as a teacher we can on one of your long school holidays have a nice holiday together perhaps in a place in Devon where we can spend time relaxing in the sunshine and have a swim together or perhaps we could make a visit to Scotland and enjoy the scenery in the Highlands and maybe see the Lochness monster or go to

Aberdeen and try to see the Northern Lights." Oh!" Said Rima, "I would like to do that I have always wanted to see the Northern Lights, I always thought the only way I would get to see them was to go to Scandinavia." Harry replied with, "I'll really enjoy taking you if that's where you would like to go, we would have much more chance of seeing the Aurora borealis as the Northern lights are called officially, than the Lochness monster which only a very few people claim to have seen and which no one is sure really exists." Harry now told Zima that she should ask a few of her friends to come to the wedding as they would need a couple of witnesses and he would arrange for a little party after wards for them at the registry office which was in a lovely former large house and had a big room for a party. Rima replied, "that is a good plan I will speak to some of my friends and ask them if they could come and let you know in a few days time." Three days later Rima and Harry met again at her flat in Woodstock and Rima told Harry that four of her friends would be coming to see the wedding and enjoy a party afterwards. Harry replied, "my uncle Ian who has helped me a lot will also be coming as Best man and also as one of the two witnesses we must have and one of your friends can be the other one so please ask them." Harry now told Rima that after the wedding she would be alright living in his house as he had changed his jobs and would be able to take her each day to Oxford and bring her back as he wasn't starting his new job for possibly a year or so. About four weeks later the marriage took place and after a very enjoyable meal and party in which a few of rima's friends from university played some Jazz music which enabled a little dancing to take place, Rima and  Harry settled in Harry's house together. Harry was now free to take Rima back and forward to Oxford for the short time until she had finished her teaching certificate. Knowing Rima was about to qualify as a teacher and when employed would have  a number of quite long holidays Harry began to think about becoming a teacher himself and wondered how he might gain entry to a college and complete a teaching Certificate perhaps he thought as a PE teacher with his knowledge of coaching sword fencing and he had also been good at cricket when in Australia and had been good at table tennis while living at home in Rhodesia. During his time working with Sir Cameron and thanks to the help of some of his colleagues he had also become a very good speaker of French. As well as having these thoughts about his future.He also began fencing with Rima again something they both enjoyed each becoming better at it than before. Harry now began to regret his past and decided he would be a good person from now on and perhaps start a family of his own. His next step was to start going to a local church of England and to encourage Rima to become a Christian and do the same, which he succeeded in doing. Rima was happy to attend services each Sunday listening to and enjoying the singing of the hymns especially. Soon she began to read her bible at home.

Attending his local Church of England and having a cup of tea with other members at the end of each service and a half hours chat with them. Encouraged Harry to become a very

 changed person and to begin to believe very much in God and the love of God in sending Jesus to earth where Jesus was killed on the cross then was buried in a cave and after three days rose again from the dead and shortly afterwards returned to heaven from where he would one day return to rule the whole world. First, Jesus sent the Holly spirit to help create faithful believers in God and through his own teaching and behaviour taught them how to behave correctly as well as to know that humans were forgiven for their sins so long as they admitted to committing them in their prayers to God as well as promising in their prayers to God that they would stop sinning and behave properly ever after and actually do this. Rima became pregnant three months after their wedding which meant the baby would be born well after she had finished her teacher training course. Then she would have to make arrangements for childcare before she could start work. Harry having got the promise of a good job, told Rima not to apply for any local teaching jobs yet until he could sort out some suitable child care for the baby when born. Which Rima agreed to do. To solve the problem Harry spoke to his uncle Ian whose own children were grown up, His Uncle after a short time in which he discussed things with his wife, told Harry his wife would be happy to come along and spend time looking after Harry's children when born and should Harry's wife find herself a job teaching. From here on Harry and Rima had a lovely time together with Rima's pregnancy developing nicely and both of them enjoying a little fencing only for a short time as Rima developed her pregnancy, they did this even though it required a fair bit of driving to get to their choice of club. When the weather was good Harry would also take Rima to a bed and breakfast house in Betws y Coed in Wales for short walks in the lower area around Snowdon which she enjoyed very much even while carrying her unborn baby. Once the child a boy was born and Harry's uncle's wife came to take care of the baby, Rima applied for teaching Jobs getting one not too far away from where they lived. Harry not as yet offered his new job, but with a fair amount saved from his job with Sir Cameron and knowing Rima had a huge amount in her savings account. Planned a trip for them, to take place during Rima's half term holiday, at the beginning of the coming month of November. The trip going to Aberdeen so that they might get a chance to see the Northern Lights. When he told Rima, she was thrilled at the possibility of completing one of the things she had always wanted to do. She asked Harry where they would be staying and he told her a bed and breakfast house in Aberdeen and that he would drive them there even though it was a long drive as that would mean they would have a car to use to view other parts of Scotland in that area, which he thought they would both enjoy. They would be able take their son Frederick with them together with his pram and back carrier straps, so Harry could carry him on his back. Harry told Rima that they would need good warm clothing for themselves as well as for their baby because the Northern Lights would only be seen after dark and Scotland could be very cold at that time of year even during the day. He also suggested that they might visit the Scottish Highlands whilst there.

Rima replied, "It sounds as if we will have a lovely time. I hope it doesn't snow or rain while we are there, so we won't have to worry too much about Frederick." Harry answered with "It might snow or rain but if we take the correct clothing for ourselves and for Freddy we will manage and still have a fun time." Rima then smiled and said, "I also think that in the future we should have two more children if we can. We should also in the future take our children on exciting holidays whenever possible." Harry replied in a supporting manner, "you will have good, frequent and long school holidays, which will give you time to do this. I hope I will be able to fit in with your holidays. We should also introduce our children to lots of different sports and other exciting activities such as the Duke of Edinburgh's Award in which to complete the cross country hill walk and camp section of the gold award they can walk in and camp in Snowdonia as I have done as part my fitness training. I would  also like us to teach them about Christianity and encourage them with their education at school. I will with pleasure try to give you two more children, hopefully boys." Zima replied yes please, "I would like boys as well. So long as we can make them behave themselves and work hard at school when they grow up, especially in their teenage years. Something I believe we should be able to do well."

Harry in the meantime had made enquiries about where he might be able to study to become a teacher so as to in future times enjoy the same long holidays as his wife and children.

Printed in Great Britain
by Amazon

13493749R00089